BE

ARROW

Skye stared at the young woman in the doorway. A cascade of deep blond hair framed a face as sensual as it was gorgeous: full, very red lips, a short, straight nose, cream-white skin and deep-blue eyes that absolutely smoldered. Her plain gray dress might have been a red satin gown as it clung to her magnificently curved, full breasts, narrowed quickly to her small waist, and rested on her long, slowly curving thighs.

"Yes?" she asked.

"Excuse me, I think I've got the wrong place," Fargo apologized. "I'm looking for a preacher lady. Name of Leah."

"I'm Leah," the gorgeous creature replied.

Fargo felt his eyebrows go higher. "Holy s--t," he heard himself mutter, and wondered if he should add hallelujah. "You're sure not what I expected."

A tiny smile parted the full, red lips. "Surprises are good for us," she said.

Feeling the heat radiating from her, Skye had a strong hunch that what was coming would be even better. . . .

THE TRAILSMAN 47

SIX-GUN
SALVATION

by
Jon Sharpe

A SIGNET BOOK

NEW AMERICAN LIBRARY

PUBLISHER'S NOTE

This novel is a work of fiction. Names, characters, places, and incidents either are the product of the author's imagination or are used fictitiously, and any resemblance to actual persons, living or dead, events, or locales is entirely coincidental.

Copyright © 1985 by Jon Sharpe

The first chapter of this book previously appeared in *Hell Town*, the forty-sixth volume in this series.

SIGNET, SIGNET CLASSIC, MENTOR, PLUME, MERIDIAN and NAL BOOKS are published by New American Library, 1633 Broadway, New York, New York 10019

First Printing, November, 1985

1 2 3 4 5 6 7 8 9

PRINTED IN THE UNITED STATES OF AMERICA

The Trailsman

Beginnings . . . they bend the tree and they mark the man. Skye Fargo was born when he was eighteen. Terror was his midwife, vengeance his first cry. Killing spawned Skye Fargo, ruthless, cold-blooded murder. Out of the acrid smoke of gunpowder still hanging in the air, he rose, cried out a promise never forgotten.

The Trailsman, they began to call him, all across the West: searcher, scout, hunter, the man who could see where others only looked, his skills for hire but not his soul, the man who lived each day to the fullest, yet trailed each tomorrow. Skye Fargo, the Trailsman, the seeker who could take the wildness of a land and the wanting of a woman and make them his own.

1860, just above Farewell Bend in
the new State of Oregon, where some came
to steal and some came to save
and the Northern Shoshoni arrows made
no distinction. . . .

1

"I'm getting the hell out of here," the big man with the lake-blue eyes muttered.

"You most certainly are not, Mr. Fargo," Rev. Joshua Johnston hissed. Fargo threw a grimace of exasperation at the man as the reverend leaned forward in the saddle, his long-tailed black minister's coat making him look like a huge crow on the horse. Rev. Johnston's long, lean face gazed down at the lone wagon rolling across the hollow of land. Fargo's eyes flicked to the line of near-naked bronzed horsemen in the distant timber as they paralleled the wagon below. "That Conestoga is going to be attacked," the minister said.

"By fifteen Northern Shoshoni. Those are no-win odds and I'm getting out of here," Fargo said.

"No, you're not. It's your Christian duty to help the people in that wagon down there," Rev. Johnston said, his long, lean face growing longer and leaner with righteousness.

"Where does the bible say a Christian has to be a damn fool?" Fargo threw back.

The reverend straightened his spare, bony frame and clutched the small, black leather-bound bible to his chest. "A Christian feels a responsibility to his fellow man," he intoned.

"I feel a responsibility to my scalp," Fargo snapped. Rev. Johnston turned his eyes back to the Conestoga, which was rolling through the hollow. "You coming?" Fargo speared.

"I am not. I am going down there to give those people whatever help I can," the minister answered.

"You can't help them, dammit. All you can do is get your hide shot full of Shoshoni arrows. It's suicide," Fargo said.

The minister shot a glance of something close to pity at the big man. "You just can't understand the power of faith, can you, Mr. Fargo? Believing will protect me. Believing, that's what matters. What do you believe, Mr. Fargo?" the minister asked.

"I believe there are too damn many idiots in this world, and I'm not going to make one more," Fargo growled. "That Conestoga down there, one wagon alone out here, that's being idiotic."

"Perhaps they trust in the Lord, too. Perhaps they believe, too, Fargo," Rev. Johnston answered.

"They won't be the first ones he's disappointed," Fargo returned, and saw the minister's eyes grow wide with shock.

"That's blasphemy," the minister breathed.

"No, the Lord doesn't reward stupidity. That's been proven plenty of times," Fargo said. Fargo glanced at the Shoshoni again. The Indians continued to filter through the trees like silent shadows, unaware they were being watched, their concentration on the lone Conestoga below. Suddenly, as one, the fifteen loinclothed riders turned their ponies and began to drift downward. "The Shoshoni have stopped watching. So have I," Fargo said.

The Reverend's eyes stayed on the wagon below as the Shoshoni came out of the timber and into plain view. "They must see those savages now," he murmured. "But they just keep rolling on at the same pace."

"It's hard to make a circle with one wagon," Fargo observed, and the bitterness laced his words. "For the last time, you coming or do you like watching a massacre?" Fargo said.

The cry from the Shoshoni swept away the Reverend's answer, and as Fargo started to send the Ovaro upward into the high timber, he saw the Indians racing their short-legged ponies downhill. He glimpsed rifle barrels being poked out from under the canvas of the Conestoga and saw the driver climb inside the body of the wagon. He heard the rifles bark, old single-shot weapons for the most part, and he watched the streaking cluster of Shoshoni peel away from one another like a sunflower peeling back its petals. Fargo continued to look back as the Ovaro climbed the hillside. He cursed as his view was momentarily obscured by long black coattails flapping across his gaze. Rev. Joshua Johnston was riding full tilt down the hill to the wagon, which had come to a stop.

"Dammit to hell," Fargo swore as he reined up in a cluster of black oak. The Reverend had almost reached the wagons, firing a big Dragoon Colt with a hell of a lot more righteousness than accuracy at the line of Shoshoni that raced around the wagon in a furious circle.

"Heathens," Fargo heard the reverend shout. "Savage heathens."

The Shoshoni answered with an arrow that

struck him right between the shoulder blades, and the minister twisted in the saddle before he fell from the horse. He landed only a dozen feet from the wagon and started to crawl toward the undercarriage when another arrow hit him, this one in the small of his back. The minister twitched in pain, lay still for a moment, and then continued to try to pull himself under the Conestoga.

"Ah, shit," Fargo swore as he slid out of the saddle and yanked the big Sharps from its saddle case. He saw the bottom edge of the canvas pulled up on the Conestoga as a man leaned out, reached down to grab hold of the minister. He stayed that way as three arrows hurtled through him to pin him to the side of the wagon, head down. A woman screamed, came half out to try to pull the man back. The arrow that plunged halfway through her abdomen knocked her back into the wagon. Fargo knelt down as he drew the Colt and held the rifle in his other hand. There was only one chance, he realized. It had worked, just as often as not, and when it didn't, you ran like hell. He fired two shots from the big Sharps, two from the Colt, another two from the rifle, and then two more fired simultaneously.

He saw the circling Shoshoni look up toward the hill where he lay as they continued their circling. He reloaded, moved a half-dozen steps to his right, fired a volley from the Colt and another from the rifle, moved back, and fired the rifle again. The Reverend had crawled under the Conestoga, he saw as the Shoshoni broke off their attack on the wagon but stayed apart to make themselves harder targets. But he was firing for effect, not accuracy, and he blasted another volley off with the rifle.

He had counted on a basic element of the Indian,

and it was working, he saw with grim satisfaction. Fearless in battle, the Indian was an instinctive tactician, always wary of being drawn into a trap by what he couldn't see, the caution ingrained in war between the tribes. Fargo watched as one of the bucks, a young figure wearing a golden-eagle feather in his brow band, waved an arm and peeled away. The others followed at once, still leaving plenty of distance between one another. The Shoshoni rode into the trees of the slope at the other side of the hollow, and Fargo watched as they made their way upward. He allowed a sigh of relief to escape his lips. They hadn't been a war party, painted up for killing on the outside and charged with it on the inside. They'd not have broken off, not this quickly. They'd been a hunting party that saw an easy mark and descended on it. But their real reason for going on had been the one echoed by the wagon as Fargo brought his gaze to focus on it. It resembled a giant pincushion on wheels. The Shoshoni had done what they'd set out to do. There'd be one less band of settlers, and they were content with that much.

Fargo stayed in place as he watched the movement of the leaves on the opposite hill and traced the Shoshoni's path over the crest. He waited further, though, watched to see if they changed their minds and circled back. But the distant foliage remained still. He rose, holstered the guns, and climbed onto the Ovaro. He sent the magnificent black-and-white-marked horse streaking downhill, out into the open land and toward the wagon. Maybe someone was still alive, still crouched in frozen fear. Maybe even Rev. Johnston, he grunted, and knew that the word maybe mocked probability.

He leapt from the horse as he reached the wagon, went to the rear of the Conestoga to peer through the eliptical opening in the canvas. He felt his jaw tighten as he saw three people, one man and two women, all dead. They and the man pinned to the side of the wagon had been the only occupants. No children, he noted, and felt grateful for that much. He always felt that way when there were no children. They were the innocents, the real victims. He stared for a moment at the three figures sprawled among the cloth satchels and bags that contained their only worldly possessions, and stepped back, went around to the side of the wagon, and dropped down to one knee to peer underneath.

Rev. Johnston lay on his side, a third arrow protruding from between his ribs. But Fargo heard the sound of rasped breathing. He reached in, pulled the minister out between the wheels. He looked at the three arrows, all deeply embedded, and wondered that the man was still alive. Then he saw the minister's eyes open. The Reverend stared at him for a long moment, and his hand slowly lifted to fasten itself around Fargo's arm. "You . . . go on, Fargo," the man said, each word a hollow rasp. "You paid . . . go on. Tell the others . . . tell Leah. She will lead now . . . tell her."

"Leah?" Fargo repeated.

The minister's eyes blinked a nod. "Leah . . . sister . . ." he breathed.

"Your sister?" Fargo asked.

"Sister of the Church . . . servant of the Lord . . . righteous woman," the Reverend gasped out. "Leah . . . all in her hands now. You go with Leah, Fargo."

Fargo felt the man's hand tighten on his arm for

a brief instant, then fall away as the minister's body sagged. The effort had drained what little life there was left in Rev. Joshua Johnston, and Fargo let the man's limp form slide to the ground.

"Damn," Fargo bit out as he stood up and his eyes swept the distant hillside out of habit. But only the swoop of a pair of tanagers broke the stillness. His mouth a hard, thin line, he forced himself not to just ride away, which is what the anger inside him pushed at him. He unhitched the two horses, tethered them on a single, long lead. They'd bring a fair price somewhere. He found a shovel hanging from the tailgate of the Conestoga and began the digging. The ground was soft, and he dug a wide grave, cursing with each shovelful of earth as the anger stayed inside him. When he finished, he buried the dead travelers and the reverend, bible on his chest, and stood before the wide, flat mound. The anger was a hard rock in the pit of his stomach. No words of solace or piety came to him, and the only words he found welled up out of the anger inside him. "I was right," he said accusingly as he stared at the far left of the wide mound where he'd placed Rev. Joshua Johnston. "He doesn't reward stupidity. Amen."

Fargo strode away, climbed onto the Ovaro, and rode north at a fast trot, pulling the two horses from the wagon behind him. He slowed when the hollow widened into a small plain dotted with clusters of gambel oaks. The town of Farewell Bend lay only a few miles north, he estimated. That's where the reverend had been headed with him when they'd spotted the lone Conestoga. The town's name held a grim appropriateness, Fargo grunted, and his lips pulled back in disgust. The thought of riding trail for some dried-up, pinch-faced, righteous, lecturing old spinster was a lot less than appealing. In fact, he had almost turned down the Reverend when the man sought him out up in Sweetbridge. Fargo recalled the meeting. He had brought Fred Ingraham's wife and two boys over the Salmon River Mountains across Idaho to Sweetbridge, and he and Fred had celebrated for two days and nights. But he'd sobered and was preparing to leave when the Reverend came up to him.

"I am Reverend Joshua Johnston, a minister of the Church of the Word," the man had said as he introduced himself. "You are Fargo, the Trailsman."

Fargo recalled tossing the minister a narrow-eyed stare. "They call me that," he had answered cautiously. "You come recruiting you're wasting your time, Reverend."

"I've come on business, Fargo," Rev. Johnston had said. "I want you to take me and my followers into the Painted Hills territory."

"Where into the Painted Hills?" he'd questioned.

"I'll tell you as we go along," the reverend had said.

"No dice, preacher. When I break trail, I want to know where, what, and why," Fargo said.

"All right, I'll give you the details when we get to Farewell Bend. My followers are waiting there for me," the minister had said.

"What kind of followers?" Fargo asked.

"Men, women, families—all believers. You can call them my disciples, apostles. We are all missionaries. We want to bring the Word to everyone, especially the heathen savages."

"They've already got their word. They'll take a lot of convincing," Fargo remarked.

"Faith will show me the way to them," Rev.

Johnston had answered, and Fargo remembered shrugging. The reverend had a right to try, he had thought. He wasn't the first to do so, and it was likely he wouldn't be the last. But sensing rejection, the minister had named his price to be paid in advance, and it had been the kind of money hard to turn down. But it had really been the letter from Tom Haydon's widow in his pocket that had decided him to take the job. Jessie had written of how desperately she needed money to save the farm back in Kansas since Tom died. He'd had the letter in his mind when he took the reverend's offer. Fargo gave a harsh grunt as he rode. He had sent the money to Jessie on the first post. There was no way for him to give it back and bow out. He had to go through with it, and he shook his head angrily at the thought. But a man had to live by his own rules, and fair was fair.

He continued north, and the day began to move toward dusk when he caught sight of the town. He sent the Ovaro into a canter, pulled the two wagon horses behind him, and slowed again when he rode into Farewell Bend. The town surprised him by being larger than he'd expected, containing a bank and a meeting hall as well as a dance hall. Deciding not to waste time searching for the reverend's followers, he halted at the town blacksmith shop.

"Mighty fine-looking horse," the smithy said with the eye of a man who knew his horseflesh.

"Thanks." Fargo nodded. "You see any church folk in town? I think there's likely to be a fair-sized group."

"Sounds like those at Emmet's Boarding Hotel," the blacksmith said. "Last house other end of town."

"Obliged," Fargo said, and moved the Ovaro on through Farewell Bend. The boarding hotel was indeed the last structure of the town, he saw as he reached it, a large, two-story clapboard building painted yellow with white trim. He halted and took in the collection of wagons drawn up on both sides on the house: two proper Conestogas, a high-sided Bucks County hay wagon outfitted with a canvas top, two Owensboro seed-bed wagons built with wooden bows for canvas tops, a big California rack-bed wagon with sides and roof of thin wood built on, and a milk wagon painted light green and with curtains on the windows. He grimaced, dismounted, and entered the boarding hotel.

A huge figure, nearly three hundred pounds, Fargo guessed, leaned against one wall inside the entrance. A mountainous, overstuffed belly strained against a white sleeveless shirt to the breaking point. Above it, huge shoulders made a fat face seem small despite its folds of flesh and hanging jowls and bald pate. Fargo saw the mountain of flesh watch him until he turned and went down a wide hallway to knock at the first door.

He heard footsteps behind the door, and then the latch turned and the door pulled open. He found himself staring at a young woman. A cascade of deep-blond hair framed a face as sensual as it was gorgeous, full, very red lips, the lower one slightly thicker than the upper, both finely molded at the edges, a short, straight nose, cream-white skin, and deep-blue eyes that absolutely smoldered. The rest of her matched the face, he noted. A gray dress of determined plainness might well have been a red satin gown on her figure as it clung to magnificently curved, full breasts, narrowed quickly to a small waist, and rested on long,

18

slowly curving thighs—a figure that sent contained sensualness in waves.

"Yes?" she asked, and the deep-blue eyes somehow managed to be cool as they smoldered.

"Excuse me, I think I've got the wrong place," Fargo apologized.

"The right place for the Lord's Word is here," she said, and Fargo lifted his eyebrows.

"It is?" he asked. "I'm looking for Leah."

"I'm Leah," the gorgeous creature answered.

Fargo's eyebrows rose higher. "Holy shit," he heard himself mutter, and wondered if he should add hallelujah. He saw a tiny layer of frost come over the smoldering eyes. "It's just that you're not what I expected," he said.

The tiny smile that parted the full red lips held both tolerance and an edge of superiority. "Surprises are good for us. They teach us caution," she said.

"Guess so," he murmured, and decided that the throbbing sensuality was tightly held under wraps. Probably damn well had to be, he told himself.

"Have you come to inquire about the Church?" Leah asked.

"I've come about Reverend Johnston," he said.

Her smile widened. "The reverend is due back today. He is our leader, you know," she said.

"Was your leader," Fargo corrected.

She caught the note in his voice, and the smoldering eyes clouded. "What do you mean?" She frowned.

"I mean he ran himself into a handful of Shoshoni arrows," Fargo said.

Shock leapt in the deep-blue eyes as she stared back. "How do you know this?" she questioned.

"I was with him. Name's Fargo . . . Skye Fargo," he said.

"You're the one he went to Sweetbridge to hire, the Trailsman," Leah said. Fargo nodded, and she pulled the door open wider, leaned back, and called into the room.

"Mishach, Shadrach," she called, "did you hear?"

Two men appeared from behind the door, each with a rifle pointed at him. "We heard," one said as the young woman stepped back. "Get in here, mister," he ordered.

2

Fargo eyed the two rifles, both big .52-caliber Spencers, and decided to do nothing. They were too close, both wouldn't miss. His glance went to the young woman as he stepped into the room. A disapproving severity came across her sensual face. "You have failed, most terribly," she said to him. "Reverend Johnston was not only our leader, but my uncle."

"What do you mean, I failed?" Fargo bristled.

"It was your fault that he was killed," she said severely.

"How the hell do you figure that?" Fargo frowned.

"You said you were there. You had been hired and paid. It was your responsibility to look out for him," the young woman said tightly.

Fargo felt the resentment spiral inside him. He debated telling her how damn stupid her late uncle had been, but decided to hold back. "I was hired to break trail not be a wet nurse," he growled. "He refused to listen to me, and he paid for it."

"Here in the Church of the Word we believe in being our brothers' keepers," she said, her smug superiority adding to his resentment.

"Hooray for you," he snapped. "The reverend told me to tell you it's all in your hands now."

The deep-blond hair fell across her face as she bowed her head. "Yes," she murmured. "I shall keep the faith, and do my best."

She stayed with her head bowed for another minute. When she lifted her head, her eyes returned to Fargo.

"Now, what?" he asked.

"We go on, of course," Leah said. "I hope you do not think this lets you out of your agreement with Reverend Johnston."

"Didn't expect it would," Fargo said.

"That shows some measure of moral responsibility," Leah said, studying the man before her. She took in the intense, chiseled proportions of his face, the strength of his features, and the power of his hard-muscled frame. "You have a strong face, Fargo. With proper discipline you could develop real moral responsibility," she commented.

"I doubt it. Looks are deceiving," Fargo said blandly. She had a way of making everything she said sound like a pronouncement. The late reverend's influence, no doubt, he mused silently.

She turned to the two men. "Put the rifles down. Mr. Fargo has seen his duty," she said, and the two men lowered the guns at once. "This is Mishach," she introduced. Fargo took the man's medium build, his half-bald head, and the hard face with deep lines around the mouth and eyes that burned with intensity. "And Shadrach," Leah said, gesturing to the second man. He had a heavier build, a face more square but no less hard, and the same intensity in his eyes. Both men nodded with stonelike expressions. "Most of the followers take Biblical names when they join the Church," Leah explained. Then she turned to the two men, and Fargo watched the gray dress stretch in round taut-

22

ness across the full breasts. "We'll have to go back, of course," she said to Mishach.

"Whatever you say, Leah." The man nodded.

"Go back where?" Fargo frowned.

"Back to where you left Reverend Johnston," she said to him. "There is something I must see to."

"I buried him," Fargo said.

"I'm glad to hear you did the proper thing," Leah said. "You said words over him, I should hope?" Fargo nodded. "Something from Ecclesiastes, I presume."

"Something appropriate," Fargo muttered.

"We shall have to unbury Reverend Johnston," Leah said.

"I don't like it," Fargo growled.

"You've a fine sense of good Christian propriety. I like that," Leah complimented.

"You've a fine way of jumping to conclusions," Fargo said. "Why do you have to go back?"

"I shall tell you that when we've finished. You can lead us back," Leah said.

"I can, but I'm not sure I will."

"It's your duty to take us back," Leah said. "Just as it is to take us forward."

Fargo's lips pressed hard against each other as he turned Leah's words in his mind. He half-shrugged after a moment. "After that?" he asked.

"We shall return here to Farewell Bend and then set out on our journey. I'll have you meet the rest of the believers tomorrow," she said as she walked to the door with him. "Welcome, Fargo. You will be one of us as we journey. It will be a time of new discovery for you."

His eyes followed the soft swing of her full, round breasts as she moved. "I'm hoping that," he agreed.

"We'll meet outside the hotel in the morning.

Good evening, Fargo," she said, and he left the room.

Leah was indeed a strange combination. There was a strong sensuality within her, that was for sure, but it was contained by something more than cool confidence, he decided. She had an almost righteous superiority about her that irritated him. Maybe all she needed was a little prodding to release that earthiness inside.

He turned the corner of the hallway and saw that the mountainous character still leaned against one wall by the entranceway. A gleam of lamplight made his bald head shine. Shadows fell along the thick folds at the back of what would have been a neck on most people.

Fargo went outside. Night had come down, and he felt his stomach nudge at him. He led the Ovaro down the main street of town and wondered idly whether the mountain of flesh was one of Leah's followers or belonged to the boarding hotel. He halted at the dance-hall saloon, dropped the Ovaro's reins over the hitching post, and went inside. He found a small table in a corner and ordered a plate of corned-beef hash, the meal of the day, and a glass of bourbon from a stooped old man. Then he sat back and watched the dance-hall girls try to coax customers into more than dancing and drinking.

The waiter brought him his order and the hash was edible, the bourbon better than he'd expected. He ordered another glass and sipped it with relish, Leah swimming into his thoughts again. She was unquestionably one hell of a piece of woman, but she seemed as zealous a believer as had Rev. Johnston. Yet it hadn't overcome that smoldering sensuality, and that was a good sign, he reflected.

Yet there was something different about Leah and her two biblically named assistants. They just didn't seem the ordinary churchgoing folks.

He drained his bourbon, ordered another, and pushed aside further thoughts. It was too early to tell whether he was in for a trail of unexpected pleasure or unexpected trouble, and whether Leah was going to be icing or ice.

One of the dance-hall girls brought his bourbon and slid an ample rear onto the chair beside him. She looked at him from beneath false eyelashes, her youth grown hard too soon. "You're new here," she said, and surveyed him with appreciation. "I like new."

"Maybe later." He smiled. There was no need to tell her she wasn't his type. And she sauntered away with an extra wiggle. He sipped the bourbon, leaned back in the chair, and enjoyed the scene in front of him as the saloon grew more crowded and extra girls appeared from a back room as if on cue.

He wasn't looking at the door, but he saw other eyes go there and he let his gaze follow to rest on the huge figure that more than filled the entrance-way. The bald head shone under the light from the overhead chandelier, the folds of fleshy jowls hanging from the flaccid face. The sleeveless white cotton shirt had ridden up so that part of the overstuffed belly showed between it and the trousers below.

Fargo saw the little eyes scan the dance hall and fasten on him. The mountainous shape immediately began to move across the dance hall toward him. The man moved in a straight line, a steady, lumbering gait, and others stepped aside the way deer made way for a buffalo. The huge figure came to a halt in front of the table. "You leave here," he said in a voice surprisingly high in pitch.

"What?" Fargo frowned. "Who are you?"

"I am Nathaniel. Leah says you leave here," the huge man repeated.

Fargo's frown deepened. "Leah says? Why?" he questioned.

"Leah says it is not right for anyone with the Church to be in a place like this," was the reply, and Fargo felt the disbelief inside him edging into anger.

"What kind of shit is this? I'm hired help," he answered.

"You have been hired. You are working for the believers. That is enough. Sister Leah says to leave here," the hulk insisted with a kind of slow-witted doggedness.

Fargo found anger crystallizing inside him. That woman had her goddamn nerve. He stared at the hulk with steel-blue eyes as a number of messages crossed his mind. He chose the mildest. "Tell Leah to get lost," he growled.

"You leave here," the hulk repeated.

"Go to hell," Fargo said, and drained his bourbon.

The huge figure exploded with astonishing quickness, and Fargo saw the buffalolike charge coming at him. Huge arms snapped out and hamhock hands closed around his shirt. Fargo felt himself fly through the air and land on the floor. He rolled, came up on his feet, and saw the hulk coming at him.

"You leave," the huge figure said, treelike arms outstretched.

"You've a one-track mind behind all that fat," Fargo snapped back, and the fat man sprang, once more with surprising speed. But Fargo was prepared this time, and he ducked the attempt to grab him again. He threw a left with all the strength of his powerful shoulder behind it. The blow hit the man right on the point of his jaw, and he staggered back as the fleshy jowls shook in a paroxysm of folds. Fargo followed with a right delivered straight into the mountainous midsection. His fist disappeared into the huge belly, and the man let out a great grunting wheeze. Fargo began another left when he saw one tree-trunk arm come up in a long arc. He twisted away but the blow caught him on the shoulder, and he felt the power of it knock him face-forward halfway across a table. He sensed the huge figure coming at him, and not looking back, he flung himself sideways off the edge of the table. As he did so, he glimpsed the hulk bringing his fist downward with sledgehammer force. The blow crashed onto the table with such power that it splintered and fell apart in two halves.

The hulk whirled, the little gimlet eyes burning with anger at having missed his target. "Old wood," Fargo said, and with a high-pitched roar of rage, the mountainous man charged him again. Fargo waited, poised on the balls of his feet, and timed another looping left that slammed into the man's jaw. The hulk slowed but not enough as weight and momentum combined, and Fargo felt the huge bulk slam into him. He went back over another table, the huge figure half over him. The hulk used his weight to pin him as he tried to close hands around his Fargo's throat. Fargo felt the huge stomach forcing the breath from him as the man bore down hard over him. He managed to get his right arm free and, without room for leverage, drove knuckles into one of the gimlet eyes. The hulk yelped in pain, his grip loosening, and Fargo twisted free. He ducked away from another sledgehammer blow, fell to one knee, but regained his feet at once.

The huge figure came at him again, and Fargo ducked a looping blow that hurtled past his ear with a rush of air. The man followed it with another that Fargo ducked as he went into a weaving crouch. He cast a quick glance half over his shoulder and saw that he was up against some tables. He measured distances as he backed another step that placed him squarely in front of one of them. He saw the gimlet eyes gleam at once, and the hulk charged as he saw a chance to pin his foe again. Fargo held his place for a split second, letting the tree-trunk arms almost encircle him, then dropped to the floor on hands and knees. He felt the heavy legs slam into him as the huge form fell over him, pitching forward at full speed. He looked up to see the hulk's chin smash solidly into the top of the table.

Fargo heard a sharp snap, more than just a broken jawbone, then saw the bald head come up and backward with a jerk. He rolled aside as the head slid from the table and the hulk fell to the floor, a motionless mountain of flesh. Fargo rose, prodded the fat with the toe of his boot, and it merely jiggled. He bent down, pushed at the heavy face, and the head rolled limply. "Neck's broken," Fargo said as he stood up, and his eyes swept the onlookers. "I want four men and a wagon. I'll pay four dollars," he said.

A portly, grizzled figure stepped forward at once. "Four dollars? You got it, mister," he said. "Be right back."

Fargo nodded, strode to the bar as two men began to pick up the overturned and broken tables as the dance hall returned to normal with determined quickness. He downed the bourbon the bartender offered, left enough coins to pay for some of the damage, and walked to the doorway.

He stepped outside as four men were bringing a one-horse Studebaker farm wagon. He watched from the side as the four went into the dance hall and dragged the huge figure out to the wagon. It took all their strength to lift him into the wagon, where he lay with the top of his belly curving up over the sides and one arm hanging loose.

"Emmet's," Fargo said, and the men climbed onto the wagon and headed for the boarding hotel. Fargo followed on the Ovaro and slid from the saddle when they drew up in front of the hotel. He paid the four men, and the portly, grizzled one questioned with his eyes.

"Hallway, first door on the right," Fargo said. "Tell her there's a package outside for her." The man nodded and hurried into the boarding hotel. Fargo faded back into the deep shadows alongside the building, scanning the wagons grouped at the sides, and returned his gaze to the front door as Leah appeared, a dark-blue robe pulled around her figure. He watched as she stared at the wagon, took a few steps closer, and halted. Her deep-blond hair glinted with shafts of gold in the light from the hotel entrance, and she turned to the grizzled figure.

"You've a cemetery here?" she asked, and the man nodded. "Bury him properly. We shall hold a service tomorrow," Leah said, reached into the pocket of her robe, and drew out two silver dollars. "This will pay for your services," she said.

The man took the coins and climbed onto the wagon where the three others waited. "We'll take care of it real proper," he said, and snapped the reins over the horse.

Fargo stayed deep in the shadows as Leah watched the wagon roll away. She turned, her face wreathed in thought. She walked slowly back into the boarding hotel, her rear pushing lovely little mounds against the dark-blue robe. Fargo stepped from the shadows after she'd left, and swung onto the Ovaro. Sister Leah had gotten the message, and that was enough for the moment.

He rode out of town and bedded down under a big white oak. He slept soundly until the morning sun woke him. He washed at a stream, breakfasted on wild plums, and rode back to town and the boarding hotel.

Leah came outside as he drew up, a tan skirt and yellow blouse fitted the sensuous body almost like a glove. With her deep-blond hair, she had the brilliance of a French marigold, the yellow blouse clinging to the full, rounded breasts with seductiveness that seemed very proper indeed. The smoldering dark-blue eyes fixed on him. "Was it necessary to kill him?" she asked.

"It worked out that way," Fargo said calmly.

"You could have done as I asked," she said.

"You've a hell of a lot of nerve, honey," Fargo returned.

"I thought you'd understand," she said.

"I did," Fargo snapped harshly. "Now we both understand."

Leah ran the tip of her tongue across the full, thrusting lower lip. The smoldering eyes flared with a moment of anger she quickly put down. Mishach and Shadrach rode out from the side of the boarding hotel and led a bay mare they handed to Leah. She swung gracefully onto the horse, the tan skirt pulling tight against a nice curve of thigh.

"We are ready," she said to Fargo, and he turned the pinto north and headed out of town. Leah came up to ride alongside while Mishach, and Shadrach stayed a distance behind. Fargo felt her eyes take in the tightness of his chiseled face as he spurred the Ovaro into a trot. "I hope you are still not bothered by last night. Let's call it an unfortunate occurrence," she said.

"Last night is history, honey," Fargo said.

"Do you always call women honey?" Leah asked with an edge of displeasure.

"Most times. Saves wear and tear on the memory," he answered blandly.

"I suggest you exercise your memory more." She sniffed.

"I'll try," he said as his eyes swept back and forth across the low hills. His jaw tightened.

"You are still upset by going back," Leah observed. "Don't be. The Lord will understand."

"And you're still jumping to the wrong conclusions," Fargo said. "It's not the Lord I'm worried about. It's the Shoshoni. They left behind a wagon filled with supplies, and two horses, which I took to town last night. But they don't know that. They'll come back for a second look."

"A minor risk. We must go back," she said loftily.

He shrugged and let his gaze continue to sweep the terrain as they rode.

"It seems to me you have always been a man of the flesh, Fargo," Leah remarked as she stayed beside him.

"I was born with it. I'm attached to it," Fargo said.

"Don't you ever think about your soul?" she questioned, a condescending loftiness in her tone that rankled.

"All the time," Fargo said. "I just don't separate my soul from my scalp. I'm not much for saving one without the other." He quickened the pace.

The sun had reached the noon sky when he rode into the hollow between the hills. The wagon was still in place, a grim monument to stupidity and savagery. He reined up and Mishach and Shadrach dismounted, each taking a short-handled shovel from their horses. "Left corner," Fargo said as they walked to the wide, shallow mound.

Leah dismounted and found a log to sit on as the two men began to dig. They had dug up most of the soft earth at the corner when Fargo noticed the little line of perspiration that appeared across Leah's finely molded upper lip. "You feeling bothered suddenly?" he slid at her.

"I do what has to be done, not because I enjoy it," she answered, her eyes on the two men as they continued to dig.

"You ever do anything you might enjoy?" Fargo asked her.

"There is enjoyment in self-discipline," Leah answered.

"I hear tell some folks like to beat themselves, too," Fargo remarked, his eyes moving past her to the hill beyond.

She didn't answer. She rose as Shadrach and Mishach stopped digging and reached down into the unearthed portion of the shallow mound. Fargo's eyes stayed on the hills a moment longer, then watched the two men as they continued to reach into the pit. Finally they stopped, pulled their arms out, and Mishach looked across at Leah.

"Nothing, nothing at all," he called out. He saw Leah's lips tighten as a frown of disappointment touched her face.

"We will have to go on with what I can remember," she said. The two men began to replace the earth they had removed, and Fargo's eyes moved past Leah to the timbered slope of the hill.

"Shit," he said softly, and Leah turned to him, disapproval in her glance. "That minor risk is here," he said, and saw her eyes widen. "Don't turn around," he said sharply, and she held still. "I count eight, moving down the hill behind you," Fargo said as Mishach and Shadrach walked to their horses, their task finished. He waited as the two men brought their mounts closer. "Shoshoni," he muttered. "Everybody mount up, nice and easy. When I give the signal, ride like hell till we reach the top of the road. We split up there." He focused on Mishach. "You'll go with Leah. They'll take after you. Find a spot to hole up and make a stand."

"Just the two of us?" The man frowned.

"That's right. I want them concentrating on you while we double back," Fargo said. "Let's go."

He swung onto the Ovaro, waiting for Leah to mount the bay mare, and slowly started up the roadway where it sloped between the hills. Out of the corner of his eye he saw the Shoshoni near the bottom of the hillside, still in the tree cover. As he reached the halfway point of the road, he rose in the saddle, brought his palm down sharply on the Ovaro's rump.

"*Now!*" he shouted as the horse streaked forward. Leah was quickest to react, he noted, and the two men brought up the rear. He flung a glance back and saw the Shoshoni racing out of the trees to the road, turning in pursuit, their high-pitched yelps carrying through the hollow of land.

Fargo reached the top of the road, veered to the left, and Shadrach followed. He saw Leah go right with Mishach almost beside her. As he raced on, the Shoshoni reached the crest and wheeled after the fleeing young woman. Fargo continued on until he was certain all the Indians had ridden out of sight. Then he reined to a sharp halt and wheeled the horse around as Shadrach followed. He cantered along the crest of land until he heard the sharp crack of rifle fire. He slowed to a trot, came into sight of the stand of granite rock formations, and slid from his horse.

The Shoshoni were climbing toward where Leah and Mishach had holed up halfway up the side of the rounded rocks. Fargo pulled the big Sharps from the saddle holster, motioned to Shadrach to circle away from him, and the man crept forward with his rifle. The Shoshoni were concentrated on their quarry, and Fargo saw four of the near-naked bucks clambering over rocks, staying down as Mishach sprayed rifle fire from where he was hunkered down in the rocks.

Fargo glanced across at Shadrach, who was waiting for his signal, and went down on one knee behind a bush. He took aim and nodded. He fired the big Sharps and saw one of the bucks twirl in a strange dance as he fell. Fargo had the rifle aimed again before the Indian hit the ground, and fired. This time the Shoshoni slammed back against the rock he had been climbing, quivered, and slid slowly down, a trail of red staining the stone behind him.

Two more of the Shoshoni fell as Shadrach's fire hit on target. Fargo saw the ones closer to Mishach come into sight, start to slip and slide down. He picked off one who came into his sight, missed another who disappeared between two pointed stones. Shadrach's fire chipped away only rock now as the Shoshoni raced for safety, taken off guard and unwilling to suffer more losses. Three arrows hurtled toward him as he fired, more as a gesture than for accuracy. He peered down to the far end of the rock formation and saw the three Shoshoni race into view on their ponies, the other horses following as they rode into the tree-covered hills.

Fargo stood up, whistled, and the ovaro trotted up to him. He put the rifle away as Leah and Mishach appeared and climbed down from the rocks. He waited as they gathered their horses and came up to him. He met Leah's eyes as she allowed a reluctant apology to swim in the dark-blue depths. "Your first lesson," Fargo bit out. "Out here there are no minor risks."

She nodded but quickly assumed the cool cloak of leadership as she spoke to the two men. "Ride on ahead of us," she said. "Get everyone ready to travel as soon as we get back to Farewell Bend."

Mishach nodded, and the men turned the horses and went off in a fast trot.

Fargo let the Ovaro walk a spell as he headed back the way they had come, his eyes scanning the hillside, but only a pair of ruffed grouse stirred the leaves. The Shoshoni had gone their way, and he let a deep breath escape him.

"Talk, honey," he said gruffly, and Leah frowned at him. "You were looking for a map or some kind of directions on the reverend. Now I want to know what this is all about."

"We are going to a chosen place," Leah said.

"In the Painted Hills," Fargo said, echoing Rev. Johnston's words. "That's the heart of Northern Shoshoni country. Who the hell chose that spot?"

"It has been given us to go there. A sign has come to us," Leah said. "I do not lie. It is a sin to lie."

"What kind of sign?" he queried.

"A sign," she said, turning aside the question, and Fargo smiled. Maybe it was a sin to lie but apparently a little evasion was permissible.

"What happens after you get to this chosen place?" he asked.

"That depends. We must try to fulfill the sign," she said, again avoiding a direct answer. "My uncle told me we would have to find a river where it forks in three places, go north from there to find a hill with an altar of stone."

"He say anything about staying in one piece?" Fargo asked wryly.

"That is why he sought you out," Leah answered.

"I'm running low on miracles," Fargo said dryly, and spurred the horse on as Farewell Bend came into view. As he approached the boarding hotel, he saw the wagons lined up end to end, small knots of people standing by each.

"We will have the strength of numbers," Leah said. "That's good, isn't it?"

"Maybe," Fargo grunted, and she frowned at him. "Ever hear of waving a red flag in front of a bull?" he said. "The Northern Shoshoni won't stand by for a group this size."

"We will persevere. It is our mission," Leah said.

Fargo sighed to himself. The Shoshoni had their own mission, he muttered silently, and drew to a halt before the wagons.

Leah swung from the bay mare, and he watched her scan the groups before each wagon. She held herself very straight, carried herself magnificently, full, round breasts thrust forward under the yellow blouse. He wondered if only he felt the sensuality of her as he watched the others gaze at her with a kind of resolute respect.

"This is Fargo, the Trailsman. He will find the way for us to the chosen place," Leah announced.

Fargo watched as the followers took in her words with unemotional, disciplined acceptance. He stepped beside her as she motioned to him.

She halted before the first wagon, one of the big Owensboro seed-bed rigs. "Zeb and Ruth Classoon," she introduced. Zeb Classoon nodded, a tall man, face and body resembling a string bean. His wife was almost an echo, Fargo saw, a tall, lean woman with a long, thin face, brown hair tightly pulled back.

Fargo followed Leah to the big Bucks County hay wagon with the built-up sides. "Zach and Eve Kurtz," she said. Zach Kurtz had a firm body and well-muscled arms despite his gray hair, gray beard, and age-lined face. Eve Kurt had to be half his age, a face made plain by inner determination, brown hair worn in tight braids around her head, and eyes that avoided direct contact.

The two Conestogas were next in line. A young man and woman stood before the first with two blond youngsters, the man clean-shaven, a face of ernest, unsmiling sincerity, his wife attractive in an equally earnest way. "The Spencers," Leah said.

"Our pleasure," the man nodded.

"Paul and Delia Tooner," Leah introduced. Three youngsters clung to the couple, two boys and a girl. Paul Tooner had the same unsmiling earnestness of the Spencers. His wife was a plain woman with round eyes that seemed to stare blankly. The California rack-bed wagon came next and along with it a middle-aged couple that wore their piety heavily draped around them. "Eb and Mary Carlton," Leah said, and Fargo turned to the last wagon, the other Owensboro seed-bed rig outfitted with canvas top and painted a dull brown. The short man before it wore a preacher's collar beneath a round, cheeky face that tried to suggest strength, but offered only indecisiveness.

"Preacher Thomas," the man said. "I've been Reverend Johnston's assistant from the first days. He was a man of infinite faith and wisdom."

"More or less," Fargo said.

"This is my daughter, Rachel," Preacher Thomas said, and Fargo's eyes went to the young, very pretty girl beside him. He was startled for a moment by her. She was as different from the others as a meadow beauty is from prairie grass. No piety, no determined self-discipline in her face, he noted. Instead, he saw hazel eyes that glowed with boldness, soft full cheeks, a little upturned nose, and lips that combined a kind of pout with an almost sly little smile. Her brown hair hung loose to her shoulders and a checked shirt rested on high, round breasts that thrust forward to echo the boldness of the hazel eyes. Rachel Thomas exuded a bouncy, restless sex from her every pore, and he

38

watched her tongue moisten her lips as the hazel eyes took in his tall, powerful frame.

"My pleasure, Rachel," Fargo said. Rachel's hazel eyes silently answered, and he wondered just how old she was. He turned away and followed Leah as she walked to the light-green converted milk wagon with the curtain windows "Yours, I take it," he said.

"I shared it with my uncle," she said soberly. "Now I'll share it with his mission. He founded our Church and made followers of everyone here. He raised me to be his disciple."

She tied the bay mare to the rear of the milk wagon and climbed to the front. She stood as she took up the reins of the horse. She turned to Fargo, and he saw the dark-blue eyes smolder. "At last we are going forward," she said excitedly.

Fargo watched the others climbing onto their wagons as he walked to the Ovaro and swung onto the horse.

"We are ready," Leah called out.

Fargo saw Shadrach and Mishach appear, take a position at the end of the wagons, their faces expressionless and edged with hardness.

The Trailsman cantered to the front of the wagons, raised an arm, and beckoned forward. As the wagons began to roll, he turned the Ovaro north by west and cast a glance back at the line of wagons that followed. He was certain of only one thing: he sure as hell didn't feel like Moses.

3

He found a place between two stands of red cedar to make camp when dark came, large enough for all the wagons to fit. He noted that everyone seemed to have an assignment, gathering wood for cooking fires, dispensing tin plates, cooking, cleaning up afterward. The meal was taken with a minimum of conversation after a blessing given by Preacher Thomas. Only Rachel tried to chatter, and when no one responded, she pouted and came over to where Fargo had seated himself at the edge of the campsite.

She sat down and he saw her round little rear fill the skirt as she swished in front of him and slid a sidelong glance at him. "Mind?" she asked.

"Be my guest," he said.

"I don't see why meals have to be taken like it was a damn monastery around here." She pouted.

"That's not what a minister's daughter ought to be saying." Fargo grinned.

The hazel eyes met his glance with boldness and almost anger. "I say a lot of things I ought not say, I guess," she answered.

"Aren't you a follower?" he asked.

"Only because of my pa," Rachel said as she finished the last of her dinner and set the tin plate aside. She leaned back on both elbows, and he decided the round, high breasts were actually fairly modest. They only seemed large because of the firm, thrusting way she had with them. "Mind if I ride some with you tomorrow?" she asked.

"Fine with me," he said, and her quick smile flashed, a hint of triumph in it, and in the hazel eyes a hint of something else. "How old are you?" he asked.

"Why?" Rachel laughed. "You don't seem the kind of man who'd care about that."

"Didn't say I cared. Curious is one thing, caring's another," he replied.

"Tell you tomorrow," she said, and rose in a quick motion that made the round high breasts bounce. She hurried away with her tin plate, her hips swaying in a very unspiritual way.

He stretched out, arms behind his head, and watched the others begin to go into their wagons. The night had grown warm, the air thick, and he felt the stickiness of it on his skin. They were just into the heavy forest country that trapped warm air in a low-lying blanket.

He saw a figure move away from the wagons and walk toward him, deep-blond hair a silvery hue under the rising moon. He rose onto one elbow as Leah reached him.

"Rachel come to you for solace?" she asked, unsmiling.

"More like company," Fargo said.

"Rachel is a challenge," Leah said. "She resists the discipline of the spirit."

"You come over here to tell me about Rachel?" he asked.

"No, I want to talk to you later," Leah said. "Where will you be?"

Fargo pointed up a low slope where the cedars were touched by the moon. "Up there," he said.

"I can find a place in one of the wagons for you," she said.

"I'll stay off by myself," he told her.

Her brows rose a fraction. "The solitary thinker?" she asked.

"The solitary listener," he said.

She took in his answer with unsmiling gravity, nodded, and returned to her wagon.

Fargo stayed a little longer, then collected his bedroll and went up on the slope. He found a shaded place that let him look down at the campsite. The night was still humid, and he stretched out and waited. When Leah failed to appear, he undressed to his B.V.D.s, kept only the bottoms on, and lay down. He had fallen half-asleep when he caught the faint sound and snapped awake, listened to the hesitant footsteps. He peered through the dark and glimpsed the blond hair. "Over here," he called, and Leah turned, following the sound of his voice.

She halted as she reached him. She took in his powerfully muscled, near-naked body, the symmetrical beauty of his frame, the hard-packed flat abdomen, and the unmistakable bulge beneath it. Her eyes finally returned to his face, and he saw her swallow hard as she summoned austere disapproval. "Modesty is not one of your attributes, I see," she said.

"I'd given up on you," he told her.

"I was delayed talking to Preacher Thomas," Leah said. "You could put something more on now."

"Not much point in that now, is there?" he answered.

"Are you trying to test my willpower, Fargo?" she asked sternly.

"I'm trying to stay cool," Fargo said.

"You revel in the flesh," Leah accused.

"And you're afraid of it."

The smoldering eyes darkened, flicked over his body again before she looked directly in his eyes. "You mistake principles for fear. Chastity is not cowardice," she said.

"It is when you use it as a shield," he said calmly.

Leah forced a look of aloof righteousness. "You do not understand the spirit, Fargo. My body is a temple, a gift. It is not to be used in self-indulgence and unbridled passions. It is to be used in the service of the Church, not in the service of pleasure."

Fargo's eyes moved across the full, round breasts under the yellow blouse, the long curve of her skirt against her thigh, the throbbing, earthy beauty of her. "Honey, you've got the wrong body for all those principles." He sighed. She frowned at him with disapproval. "What'd you come to talk about?" he asked.

"Time," Leah said. "It is very important we reach our destination quickly."

Fargo feigned surprise. "I'd think chosen places would wait," he commented.

"Time is important," she said again doggedly.

"Why?" he asked almost harshly.

"There are reasons."

"More signs to find?" he pressed.

"Perhaps," she answered, her lips thinning into a tight line. She was evading again, and he let her as he smiled to himself. When the time was right, he'd pin her down. Perhaps in more ways than one, he hoped. Leah met his thoughtful gaze, her face set with determination. "I came to tell you not to be afraid to set a hard pace for us. We will be equal to it. Reverend Thomas and I agreed on that. Do not spare us," she said.

"Never spare people, only horses," Fargo told her, and pushed himself to his feet.

Leah looked away at once and kept her eyes peering into the darkness. "You are also a challenge, Fargo," she said. "But I am certain that when this trail is ended you will be a different person with different values."

"Funny, I was just thinking the same thing about you," Fargo replied. Her eyes flicked to him, lingering until she pulled her glance away angrily. She strode off without a reply and without looking back, and he chuckled as she disappeared down the slope.

He lay back down and thought back to what Rev. Johnston had said about a river that forked in three places. Probably the lower reaches of the Deschutes, where it ran through the Painted Hills, he figured. Leah and the others were more than simply earnest, more than dedicated, he had decided. They had a strange way about them, a grim kind of zealousness that bothered him. He decided it might be well to know more about the unsettling band of pilgrims he was leading to a chosen place that the Northern Shoshoni might already have chosen for themselves. He turned on his side and slept until the morning sun woke him with its warmth.

He peered at the campsite below as he dressed. Everyone was kneeling in a circle around Leah, Rachel at the farthest end. As he walked down the slope, he heard the murmur of voices. The circle broke up as he reached the campsite, and everyone rose to their feet and began to drift to their wagons.

"Our morning prayer service. You must join us tomorrow," Leah said to him. "I should like to pray for your soul, Fargo."

"Wouldn't be right, us praying for opposite things," he said.

"Meaning what?" Leah frowned.

"You praying for my soul and me praying for your body." He grinned.

She turned from him and walked stiffly away as Mary Carlton handed him a biscuit and a mug of coffee. His smile of thanks drew no more than a nod of acknowledgment. He finished the coffee, and the woman took the mug from him at once with silent efficiency. He saw Mishach and Shadrach saddling their mounts and sauntered over to the two men. "You planning to ride rear guard again today?" he asked.

"Unless you've some objections," Mishach said.

"No," Fargo answered. "You boys do much wagon-train riding?" Both men shook their heads as they finished tightening cinches. "What did you do before you joined up with Reverend Johnston?" Fargo asked.

He saw both men's face tighten at once. "That was another lifetime," Mishach answered. "When we joined the Church we became different men in a different world. The old one's gone. We don't think about it or talk about it."

"A real break with the past," Fargo said.

"Much more than that. A break with the past is for ordinary people. Followers of the Church of the Word are in a new and special life. We have been given the truth and the mission to carry the

Church forward," Mishach said, his voice taking on a ringing tone as he swung onto his horse.

Fargo glanced at the other man and saw his face had taken on the same expression of zealous determination. "There is no yesterday. There is only tomorrow and the work of the Church," Shadrach said.

Fargo nodded, pulled himself onto the Ovaro, and moved the horse to the edge of the campsite. He raised his arm, and the wagons began to roll after him. Leah maneuvered the light-green milk wagon into the center of the line, he noted, and he rode past the dull brown seed-bed Owensboro, noting Preacher Thomas's soft, round face atop the driver's seat. Rachel was still inside the wagon, he surmised, and he rode on, past the Kurtzes' Buck County hay wagon in the lead.

Fargo rode on along the trail that led between two thick stands of forest timber. The trail ran straight but soon became overgrown with vines as he went on. He slowed, letting the pinto pick its way over the thick tendrils. The land rose, became a sloping trail, and the vines suddenly gave way to thick bromegrass. He paused, peered ahead, and saw the trail continue to rise in a fairly straight line.

He heard the horse coming up behind him and turned in the saddle to see Rachel cantering up to him. She slowed to a halt beside him, and he saw she had tied the checkered shirt up by the tails to give herself a bare midriff. Fargo took in the tanned skin, young, firm, the edge of her belly button showing over the top of her riding skirt. Her hazel eyes danced as she held his gaze. Rachel, he decided, not only could but would happily talk about the others. She was plainly more interested in herself than the mission.

"Leah approve of that outfit?" he asked with a slow smile.

"I didn't wait around to ask," Rachel said, and her little smile was full of sly meanings. "You don't know how glad I am that you're here," she said. "Maybe this trip will be worth it, after all."

"You sound as though you're not excited about reaching the chosen place or the mission of the Church," Fargo remarked.

"You can say that again. I wish my pa had never joined up with Reverend Johnston." Rachel glowered. She stretched in the saddle and her breasts pushed hard against the shirt just over the bare midriff.

"What was your pa before he joined up with Reverend Johnston?" Fargo asked.

"He was a Methodist minister," Rachel said.

"Why didn't he stay one?"

"It seems they put him in a terrible place, the poorest congregation in six counties, and then expected him to produce cash and converts. He was at a dead end, and Pa isn't a strong man," Rachel said. "When Reverend Johnston came along, he just preached Pa into joining him. You didn't really know Reverend Johnston. He was a real spellbinding preacher man. He could turn a stone into a believer."

"He convinced himself into a bellyfull of Shoshoni arrows," Fargo grunted.

"I guess maybe preaching and being smart don't always go together," Rachel said, and Fargo nodded his agreement as his eyes swept the trees ahead and those on both sides of the trail.

"If your pa's better off here, then it was a good move for him," Fargo said.

"He's not. It's the same dead end. He won't take over top spot. Reverend Johnston turned it all over to Leah, you saw that yourself," Rachel said. She paused and frowned into space. "I don't really blame him for that. She's strong. That's what he wanted: somebody strong and all fired-up with the Church as he was."

"What do you want, Rachel?" Fargo asked.

Her smile was suddenly full of very womanly wisdom. "To live. To feel outside all the things I feel inside," she said. "And one day, to get away from all this." She rubbed the skin around her bare midriff with one hand, a slow, surprisingly erotic movement.

"You were going to tell me how old you are," he reminded her.

"Old enough to want," she said with a sudden burst of half-anger and half-hunger.

"If you're playing games with me, you could get burned, honey," Fargo said.

"I'm not playing games," Rachel answered quickly.

"Why me?" he asked.

She made a wry face. "You don't think any of these holier-than-thou characters would do anything, do you?" she said. "Besides, they'd be afraid of Leah. You don't look like the kind of man who'd be afraid of anything much."

Fargo let his eyes continue to sweep the terrain as he digested her words. "I could be persuaded," he said finally. "But how come you're so different, especially being a preacher's daughter?" he questioned.

"I lived with my ma until she died three years

ago. She and Pa had been separated for ten years. He took me in then, but I never did fit what he and Reverend Johnston expected. They made me a member of the Church, a follower, and they said I'd come around to being a true believer in time," Rachel said.

"I don't see much sign of that," Fargo commented dryly.

"That makes two of us," she said as Fargo pulled up to a stream that bubbled its way across the trail.

He dismounted, let the Ovaro drink, and Rachel slipped from the saddle. She took a handful of the cool water, rubbed it over her neck and down her chest, her fingers reaching deep inside her blouse as she watched him watching her. He smiled inwardly. Rachel didn't try to mask anything with coyness, her actions bold and honest. There was nothing calculated about her, he concluded, only the natural provocativeness of a young, ripening woman. "What do you know about the others?" he asked.

"Why?" she returned, instantly picking up the unsaid in the question. He laughed softly. Rachel was all instinct.

"Somethings don't set right with me. Can't pin them down yet," he said.

"I know enough," she told him.

"You going to tell me?" he asked.

"That depends," she answered, and he waited. "You give me what I want, and I'll give you what you want," she finished. She leaned back, and the bare midriff grew wider as the shirt rose up. The fleshy curve at the bottom of one breast edged into view under the shirt.

"Why not?" Fargo said. It wasn't gentlemanly to turn away a young woman panting for it the way

Rachel was, especially when he couldn't lose either way.

"I'll come visit tonight," Rachel said. "If I don't, it's because I couldn't get away."

"Don't take chances. I can wait," Fargo said.

"I can't," Rachel snapped back as the first wagon came into view.

Fargo rose, moved aside so two wagons could line up side by side for the horses to drink. When they finished, the first two wagons crossed the stream. Fargo rode on ahead again, Rachel beside him as he put the pinto into a fast trot. He reached the crest of a low rise and his gaze held on the tracks that crossed the rose.

"Shoshoni ponies, five of them," he said, the hoofprints still fully formed and moist in the ground. "Maybe two, three hours old," he said, and scanned the far slopes again. Only the swoop of a red-tailed hawk disturbed the trees. The trail went over the crest and down the other side, he saw, and stayed narrow, both sides thick with timber.

He'd gone another mile or so down the slope when the trail suddenly fell away to become a steep, sharp drop. "Damn," he muttered as he took in the angle of the drop. He scanned the thick tree growth on both sides. They were committed. There was no place to turn around even if he wanted to do so, and he swore again under his breath.

"They'll never make this," Rachel said.

"They'll make it. They have to," Fargo said, and looked past the bottom of the drop. The trail leveled off as it continued on through the heavy forest growth on both sides. He turned the Ovaro to one side and waited as the lead wagon came into sight, the Spencers' big Conestoga, and right behind it, Eb Carlton's California rack-bed rig. The other wagons came up, halted single-file, and he saw their occupants swing to the ground and hurry forward to see why the line had stopped. Leah came up, frowned down at the edge of the steep drop. Shadrach and Mishach edged their horses past the wagons to come up.

"Impossible," he heard Mishach mutter.

"No," he said. "One wagon at a time. Driver on the handbrake, two men at each rear wheel. Let's go." He positioned himself to the side, where he had a clear view of the entire length of the drop, and watched the first Conestoga start down. Spencer pulled with all his strength on the hand brake, and the four men at the back wheels dug heels deep into the ground as they pulled hard on the big wheels. The Conestoga half-slid, half-rolled by inches, but it finally reached the bottom of the drop and moved away as the men climbed back to take on the second Conestoga. Once again, the big wagon slid slowly down, and when it reached the bottom, Fargo had the men rest before letting the Classoons' Owensboro seed-bed rig go down.

It was the Carltons' California rack-bed that suddenly started to go out of control, its hand brake too small to be of much use and its weight poorly distributed on the frame.

"I can't hold her," Fargo heard Zeb Classoon shout and saw one of the men at the rear go down.

"Ropes," He yelled at Mishach as he spurred the Ovaro forward. He whirled his lariat to hook onto a corner of the front part of the wagon frame. He saw Mishach take the other side and hook his lariat across the opposite corner. Wrapping the rope around the saddle horn, Fargo moved the Ovaro backward as Mishach did the same with his horse. The big wagon slowed its slide and almost came to a halt.

"All right, start easing her down again," Fargo said. "Real slow now." He felt the Ovaro dig its legs into the ground as the horse used its powerful hindquarters to pull back until the wagon finally reached the level ground below.

Fargo and Mishach had to use the ropes again as Leah started down. She had the lightest of all the wagons, but it too had a poor hand brake and was too high, with a poor center of gravity. It almost went on its side twice before they managed to get it down safely. The other wagons came down with sweat and hard work but with no more near disasters, and Fargo followed the last down to where the others had halted in line on the trail below. Rachel beside him, he halted at Leah.

"I'll scout on farther ahead from now on," he said. "We got away lucky this time."

"It was believing and the mission of the Church that made us prevail," Leah said.

"It was my know-how," Fargo snapped. "You'd all have been in pieces at the bottom otherwise."

"Yes, but the mission of the Church is what brought you here and why you made it work. It is believing. You are here because you are supposed to be here," Leah said with lofty patience.

"What happens when it doesn't go right? Reverend Johnston believed," Fargo returned.

"Then it wasn't meant to happen," Leah said, and Fargo frowned back at her.

"Neat," he said. "Does away with all personal responsibility, doesn't it?"

"My personal responsibility is to see to the mission of the Church," Leah said.

"I'll try to take care of the details," he tossed back, and sent the Ovaro into a canter down the trail. He rode on, shaking his head at the exchange with Leah.

The trail stayed level and the trees leaned in from both sides. He slowed as he heard Rachel hurrying after him, and she laughed as she came alongside. She seemed a breath of fresh air, and he suddenly understood her more than he had at first.

"Could have told you you wouldn't like Leah's way of seeing things," Rachel said.

"It's got to be hard to live with that kind of reasoning. They've an answer no matter how much sense you toss at them," Fargo said.

"Too hard," Rachel said. "For me, anyway."

Fargo rode on, quickened his pace as he saw the first signs of dusk starting to tint the sky. He spotted a small lake nestled atop a hillside—too steep for wagons but not for people. He spotted a good place to camp at the bottom of the rise, and the lake above it was almost screened from sight by a stand of balsam. He rode into the place and dismounted, tethered the Ovaro, and scanned the surrounding terrain again. He saw nothing to bother him and turned to Rachel as she came to stand in front of him.

"How long before they get here?" she asked, and her breasts almost touched his chest.

"Not long enough." He laughed. A half-pout came across her face as he sat down on a flat stone to find her beside him, arms sliding around his neck. "I said not long enough," he told her.

"Just a sample," Rachel murmured, and her lips were on his, soft and warm, sweet pressure against his mouth. His tongue touched her lips and he heard her murmured gasp. "Oh, God," Rachel said, and pressed herself against him. His hand closed around the smooth skin of her bare midriff, and she almost jumped as she shuddered and squealed in delight. Her hand came against his, pressing his hard into her skin, and again she gasped. He let her hold him until he pulled away abruptly. "What is it?" Rachel asked in protest.

"The wagons," he said. He saw disbelief in her eyes, then awe as the first Conestoga came into sight. Fargo rose, waved the wagon forward to the place he'd picked as a campsite for the night. He muttered to Rachel out of the corner of his mouth. "I'll be up by the lake later on," he said, and she nodded and hurried to the dull-brown seed-bed wagon as Preacher Thomas drove into the camp.

Leah drove her converted milk wagon to a halt along the far side of the site and swung to the ground.

Fargo gestured to the line of balsams on the hill. "Lake up there behind the trees. Perfect for a bath and a swim," he said. "Ladies first."

"Very good," Leah answered. "We can get supper ready while the men go up afterward. I'll tell the others."

Fargo watched her hurry to the other wagons, her full figure moving with sensual grace. He unsaddled the Ovaro as he watched Leah and the other women climb the hill to the lake above. He frowned. Something was bothering him again. It had been doing so for days, a nagging, rankling feeling he couldn't pin down, and now it had surfaced again. He turned away and proceeded to give the Ovaro a thorough brushing.

He had just finished when the women came down from the lake, Leah in the forefront brushing her deep-blond hair, the others following, Rachel

54

tagging along last. He took a towel from his saddle-bag and went up the hillside with the men. He stripped as he reached the lake and dived into the water. The lake cooled as it refreshed. He washed off the saddle dust and dived underwater, frolicked, and came up for air.

The dusk was deepening quickly as he climbed onto the shore and started to dry himself. His eyes swept over the others and it struck him again, the same nagging feeling, only now it suddenly took shape. The men had bathed in almost total silence. They never smiled, none of them, and his thoughts leapfrogged backward. He'd never seen a damn smile from any of them, not from Leah, not from any of the others. Except for Rachel, he grunted. That's what had pushed at him as he'd watched the women go up to the lake. He'd expected excited chatter, sounds of anticipation, maybe even a few giggles. But they had marched off in silence. No smiles. They were all so damn grim. Shit, Fargo muttered to himself. Wrong. All wrong, all of it.

He strolled to where Mishach and Shadrach were getting into their underwear as they sat at the edge of the lake. He frowned again as he stared at their legs just above the ankles. The lines were there, two inches or so in width, not just a place that wasn't tanned, but a roughened area of the skin, marks that would never go away. He'd seen them before, on men who had worn leg irons for years.

He forced the frown from his brow and walked on to the slope and started down the hill, putting aside what he had seen until he had another chance to talk to Rachel. He reached the campsite, Zeb Classoon and Zach Kurtz close behind him,

the other men following. The women had prepared a simple but filling meal of hash and beans.

Leah came over to him as he sat alone and ate. "I
saw that Rachel spent the entire day riding with
you," she said.

"She seems lonely," he said.

"Of course she'd choose you," Leah said, and he
saw the faint hint of disdain. "It never ceases to
amaze me how those of little dedication always
find someone like themselves."

"Maybe she hasn't got your kind of dedication.
That doesn't mean she hasn't any," Fargo replied.

"Oh, but it does," Leah said. "Without discipline there is no dedication. Without dedication
there is no mission."

"Exactly what is this mission?" Fargo asked
with more impatience than he'd intended.

"To spread the teachings of the Church, by word
and by example. To carry the gospel to all the corners of the earth," Leah said, her tone taking on the
ring of pronouncement. She stood very straight,
and her full, deep breasts pushed hard against the
top of the dress.

"To spread the gospel," Fargo echoed.

"And fight the sins of the flesh," she added.

"I expect we won't agree on what they are,"
Fargo remarked mildly.

"The difference is that I know what they are. I
don't need agreement," Leah said severely. "I
know because I understand, and you do not."
Fargo shook his head at the absolute certainty she
put forth. She reached out and took his emptied
plate. Her lovely face and the full, sensual lips
remained severe. "It's not good for Rachel to ride
with you," she said. "You represent the wrong
things for her."

"I'd say that's for her to decide," Fargo answered calmly.

"I'll remind you that my wishes are obeyed here," Leah said.

"Is that an order?" Fargo asked, and she nodded. "Then I'll remind you of the last messenger who carried your order, fellow named Nathaniel," Fargo said.

Leah's smoldering eyes held a hint of exasperation. "I've come to realize that you are a difficult man, Fargo," she said. "But you have a soul. I shall keep trying to reach it."

"Try smiling," Fargo shot out.

She halted as she started to turn away, and peered hard at him. "The Lord's work is serious," she said.

"Hell, it ought to be fun," Fargo barked. "Believing doesn't have to be so damn grim. You talk about souls? You've got a rope and halter on yours, honey. You're all wearing one. Joy to the world, that's the message, honey. That's what the good book says. Joy to the world. Nectar, not lemon juice. Open up, not dry up."

She stared at him, shock in her face, and he saw her swallow hard. Her tongue came out to wet the full lips that had gone dry. It was as if he'd struck her, and in a way he had, Fargo realized. He'd hit the very core of all she believed, everything she had been preached into believing.

Leah stared at him, her lips parted. "You don't understand," she murmured as she started back from him. "You don't understand." She turned, almost running, but held herself rigidly instead.

"Read the words again, honey. Read them right," he called after her as she disappeared into her wagon and pulled the tail door closed. Fargo turned away. He almost felt sorry for her. Maybe it would open her eyes, he pondered, make her take another look at what she went around preaching. He wasn't about to bet on that, though. He grabbed his bedroll and started through the night up to the lake.

He spread the bedroll near the water's edge, where the lake cooled the warm night air somewhat. He undressed, lay down almost naked, and peered up at a star-filled sky. The half-moon hung in one corner suspended on invisible strings.

Deer came to the lake to drink, silent forms that appeared out of the night and vanished just as suddenly. A not-so-silent drinker proved to be a big, buck elk, which lumbered away through the brush when he'd had his fill. The howl of timber wolves echoed from across the hills. The buzz and hum of insect wings and the hoarse croak of bullfrogs across the lake sounded a soothing chorus around him. The half-moon had moved higher into the blue velvet sky when he heard Rachel's voice, a half-whispered call, and he pushed himself to his feet.

She saw him and came through the balsams. He watched her eyes move up and down his near-maked, hard-muscled body. She held a tan robe clutched around herself, and he took her hand and led her to the bedroll as she stared at his body, her eyes fixed on the bulge inside his underwear. He sank down on the bedroll and gently pulled her with him. Rachel fell to her knees, shook her shoulders, and wriggled out of the robe to face him completely naked. He took a moment as she waited, her head lifted upward and her eyes closed, to enjoy the excitement of her.

Rachel was all young, firm flesh, her body

rounded, curved smoothly flowing from the nicely shaped high breasts. Her nipples were such a light pink they seemed almost white in the moonlight. Her slightly convex little belly was also smoothly curved. Below it was her curly triangle, densely black. From it flowed smooth lines of young, firm, unblemished thighs, rounded knees, and strong young calves. Her fresh body seemed to glow with youthful eagerness, and her lips parted as she kept her eyes closed. He leaned over, pressed his mouth to hers, and her arms flew around his neck.

"I've been burning up waiting to come to you," Rachel said breathlessly through feverish kisses. "Burning up."

He fell back onto the bedroll with her and pressed her breasts against his nakedness as he shed the last piece of underwear. "Ah . . . aaah . . . ah, Jesus," Rachel cried out at his touch, and her hands flew across his back, along his shoulders, down to the firmness of his buttocks.

"Oh, God," she cried out again as she responded to touch, feel, every tactile sensation with quivering, shuddering pleasure. She kissed his lips, letting her tongue flick in and out. Then she put her face to his chest and kissed his powerful pectoral muscles. She ran her lips down along his abdomen and let her hands explore his hips, the hard flatness of his belly. She hesitated a moment, then grabbed down at him, found him, and groaned achingly. Her hand gripped around him hard; her fingers pressed into his pulsating, warm maleness.

"I've wondered for so long, so long . . ." Rachel cried, breathlessly.

Fargo pulled one breast deep into his mouth. "Yes, Yes, yes," she gasped. "I love it. Oh, yes." He caressed the light-pink nipple with his tongue, drew a moist little circle around its circumference. He had to hold her down with his other hand as she squirmed wildly in delight. He brought his body over hers, and Rachel's firm, young thighs flew open, and he felt the wetness of her against his groin. He wanted to go slowly, gently with her, but she's have none of it as he rubbed his organ against her convex little belly.

"Give me, Fargo, give me. I want you now," she almost screamed in his ear. She pushed her pelvis up against him, the young, smooth thighs opening and closing against him with their own insistent message.

Her demanding desire was beyond resistance, and he felt himself rising quickly to a climax, her wild eagerness carrying him along with it. He drew back and plunged slowly but firmly into her. Rachel screamed, but if there was pain in the sound, the ecstasy drowned it out. She rose with him, thrust up as he plunged firmly. Once more her cried echoed through the trees. Her fingers dug into his back, then moved down to press into his buttocks, rake his sides. He began to plunge harder and faster into her very wet warmth. Growing close to a climax, he tried to slow, but Rachel dug harder into him with her fingers and pushed her round little belly up against him.

He felt her suddenly tighten around him, a quick, almost fleeting grip that she relaxed and then tightened again. He saw her eyes open wide. "I . . . I . . . I'm running away," Rachel cried out, wild ecstasy shining in her eyes. "Running away." He felt her stiffen, her back arch, his own rigid hardness exploded within her. A wild cry erupted from her, a cry that carried the mystery of the unknown and the ecstasy of discovery all wrapped together. Her hands clutched his shoulders and her young, firm body pumped with wild abandon with her every contraction as she continued to stare wildly at him.

"Oh, oh, oh," Rachel gasped out as she hung in the void of ecstasy with him.

Slowly he felt her body start to relax, and she sank onto the bedroll with her thighs still around him, her hands still clutching his shoulders. He saw her blink as she began to reenter the ordinary world, and her arms encircled his neck as he lay atop her. "Everything. Everything and more," she whispered against his cheek. "Except not enough."

"It never is," he told her as she let her legs fall open and stretch out beneath him.

"I want more, Fargo. Please," she murmured, and he pressed his face between her breasts. "Ooooh, yes," Rachel said, and her back arched at once. He let his hand move down her body, touching and exploring the sweet, firm youth of her. Rachel make little gasping sounds at every new place he touched. She pushed at his hand as he came to the soft, fleshy rise of her pubic mound. She pressed him down hard against her, and his fingers curled through the dense, black triangle. Rachel cried out in delight.

The eager hunger of her swept over him again as her legs opened and closed around him and her rounded little body moved back and forth and from side to side. He clasped his hands under her rear, pressed, and she cried out at the sensation. He slid his hands slowly from the two round mounds, drew them along the back of her thighs, and she cried out again.

"Please, don't make me wait," Rachel pleaded

as she pushed her pelvis upward. He rose up, ready again for her hungering demands, and thrust into her waiting portal. She half-screamed at once, came around him, and her breasts bounced as she bucked and pumped under him, hurrying the ecstasy, her churning desire consuming her.

He would have liked to slow her, to teach her the pleasures of ecstasy prolonged, but she was not ready for that yet. She had built up too much desire to appreciate the subtleties of lovemaking, he realized.

He quickly felt himself spiraling with her wildness. He thrust deep into her as she climaxed, held there, and this time her cry was a groaning sound that seemed to tear from some deep well inside her. When he finally slid down to lay beside her, she turned, drew herself half over him, and rested one round, firm breast into the little hollow of his collarbone.

"I don't want to leave," Rachel murmured. "I don't want to do anything anymore, ever but make love."

He laughed, and caressed her little round rump with his hand. She pressed herself hard against him. "You sure worked up a good case of wanting," Fargo murmured.

Rachel lifted her head and frowned at him. "I know," she said. "Maybe it was my way of fighting back against all that praying and bible reading and turning inside yourself my pa's had me do for three years. The more he kept teaching me to fight sin, the more I kept thinking about it."

"Maybe," Fargo said. "Could be part of it, but only part of it." Her eyes questioned, and he finished it for her. "Not everyone or everything is the same. There are hills and there are volcanoes."

She giggled and snuggled even closer against him. Beyond her rounded shoulder, he saw how far the moon had traveled across the late night sky. "You were going to talk to me," he said. "But you'd better get back. We can talk when you ride with me tomorrow."

"Yes, I promise," Rachel said, hugging him, rubbing her smooth young body across his. "I couldn't talk now, anyway. I'm too tingly sleepy."

Fargo rolled over, took her with him, and pulled her to her feet. He scooped up the robe and put it around her. "Go, or you'll never get back tonight. You're a real little vixen." He laughed.

"Tomorrow night?" Rachel said.

"If you can get away," Fargo answered.

"I'll get away," Rachel said with newly inspired determination. She kissed him again, a brief, soft kiss, and he watched her hurry down the hill. The moon was edging toward the dawn sky when he closed his eyes to sleep. A few hours of sound sleep would do him, he knew. But it had been in a good cause. Rachel had been close to exploding. She needed it, and he needed some straight answers. The night had been well-spent.

4

He refused to get up with the first rays of dawn and gave himself another hour of sleep. When he finally rose, the sun was out, and a white-winged dove watched him as he washed with water from his canteen and dressed. He carried his bedroll down the hillside and walked into the camp to see the morning prayer circle still in session. He had finished saddling the Ovaro when it ended, and he saw Leah come toward him, her eyes dark and full of anger. Her heels dug into the ground as she marched toward him. He liked the way her full, round breasts and cascade of deep-blond hair swayed together in rhythm.

"Over here," she hissed as she passed him to halt in a small, green alcove of paper birches. More curious than bothered, he sauntered after her. She stood very straight as she waited for him. He recognized the barely contained fury in her eyes and wondered if he was in for another bout of righteous anger.

"You steamed over the things I said to you last night?" he asked.

"Not things that were said but things that were done," she flung at him. "Rachel, that's what. Rachel."

His brows lifted. "Been doing a little churchly spying?" he answered.

"I happened to be up when she came back to her wagon," Leah said. "I confronted her."

"Why?" Fargo asked mildly.

"I had to know," Leah hissed. "She is only fifteen, Fargo."

"Old enough." He shrugged.

"Fornicating, right under my very nose, right here on this mission of the Church," Leah half-shouted. "Making a mockery of everything we stand for, engaging in a spectacle of sinfulness."

"Hold on, honey. We didn't exactly sell tickets," Fargo protested.

"But you did it. You both violated the very spirit of the Church. She came to you, she admitted that to me. But a man of goodness would have sent her away."

"The name's Skye Fargo, honey, not Saint Fargo," he said.

"You are becoming a terrible disappointment to me," Leah said.

"That goes both ways," Fargo returned. "I suppose you told Preacher Thomas."

"I did, of course. He is filled with shame. He, too, feels betrayed."

"Get off it, honey. Rachel did nothing that wasn't natural. You want to make it a sin, that's your problem," Fargo snapped.

"You simply don't understand. The sinner cannot see the sin. But it was done, and that can't be changed. I want you to pay attention to what you were hired to do and nothing else."

Fargo's eyes narrowed. "The one doesn't affect the other. You've been getting your money's worth," he returned.

"Then let's move on. Time is still terribly important. Nothing's changed about that," she said, and strode away.

He frowned as he swung onto his horse. Time again, he murmured silently. The emphasis on time just didn't fit with finding a chosen place.

He moved the Ovaro out onto the trail and saw the Carltons' big California rack-bed wagon move into the lead, Leah swinging into next in line. He watched the other wagons take their places, the dull brown seed-bed rig last in line. Preacher Thomas drove with his head bowed so low it seemed he could hardly see the road ahead. Rachel was not in sight, obviously staying inside the wagon. It was best she stay low for the morning, at least he figured. It never made sense to rub salt in an open wound. She'd find a way to come to him by night, he was confident of that.

He spurred the pinto on. Passing the line of wagons, he glanced at Leah as he rode by. But she kept her eyes straight ahead. Even the tight anger in her face couldn't completely cloak the sensuality of her, he noted as he sent the Ovaro into a canter.

He turned northwest with the path that skirted the high lake. A line of hills appeared in front of him, jutting up one after the other in an uneven procession. But none seemed insurmountable, and the passage that led over them was the only one he could see. He rode on farther, and his gaze swept the hills. Each had plenty of tree cover, mostly cedar and cottonwood, and on the ground he spotted enough Indian pony tracks to make him grimace. But he decided to go on through the hills. The Shoshoni were all over the region and would spot them sooner or later, if they hadn't already done so.

He retraced steps to make sure the wagons had swung onto the passage, then rode on again. The first hill proved easy enough, the passage straight and the slopes gentle. The second hill was just as problem-free, and he rested the horses for ten minutes before continuing.

They had reached the flattened top of the third hill and the sun had gone well into midafternoon when he suddenly came upon the gray-white, wide ribbon of water. It stretched across in front of him, perhaps thirty yards wide. He moved closer and saw the reason for its grayish-white color. The riverbanks were lined with gray clay, crumbly under the Ovaro's hooves, and the water itself sluggishly carried the gray stuff with it from farther up in the hills to the east.

He made a face. Not much depth to the gray-white water, but the crumbly clay of the banks would be soft at the bottom of the river. He sent the horse into the water and instantly felt the softness of the bottom as the horse pulled its feet up with extra effort. He picked his way across the river and found it softest in the center.

If the wagons were to make it, they'd have to cross fast and light, he realized grimly, and his gaze followed the sluggish gray-white ribbon as far as the eye could see. There was no way around it that wouldn't take days. He crossed back to the other bank, dismounted, and sat down to wait. The Carltons' California rack-bed finally rolled into view and came to a halt at the bank. Fargo rose as Leah drove the converted milk wagon alongside. He waited till the others had all come up to line the bank before he faced them.

"The bottom is soft clay. Worse than mud because if you sink deep enough there'll be no pulling you out," he said. "The only way the wagons will make it is to cross quick and light. That means everybody out, along with everything heavy—trunks, chests, whatever. Only the driver crosses with each wagon. Get to it."

He stepped back and watched the wagons disgorge passengers and then over a dozen trunks and overloaded wooden chests.

"How do we get our things across?" Zeb Classoon asked him.

"Horseback. Two riders carrying a trunk between them can make it," Fargo answered. He walked along the line of wagons poised at the bank and halted at Preacher Thomas' dull-brown rig. "I said everybody out. That means Rachel, too," he growled. The man turned helpless eyes on him, and Fargo frowned. Leah's voice was suddenly at his elbow, and he turned to see that she had followed him down the line of wagons.

"Rachel's not there," she said.

The frown dug itself deeper into Fargo's brow. "What do you mean she's not there?" he questioned.

"She is not in the wagon," Leah said firmly.

"Where the hell is she?" Fargo barked.

"She was left behind," Leah said. "Cast out, if you prefer."

Fargo felt incredulousness flood his face. "Left behind? Where? When?" he pressed.

"Before we left in the morning. She was taken into the woods," Leah told him, her face staying firmly severe.

Fargo stared at her. She somehow managed to look as though she was convinced she'd done the right thing. "I'm hearing you. I'm just having trouble believing it," he said.

"She sinned. Against right, against the teaching

of our Church, right here in the midst of this sacred mission. She has become an instrument of evil. She chose you this time, but who knows what she would have done next. A bad seed must be cast out," Leah said.

Incredulousness still surging through him, Fargo turned to the huddled figure atop the wagon. "And you went along with this, you weasel in a preacher's coat," he said, outraged.

All the man's weakness hung in his round face. "Wickedness is not less so because it is found close to one, as Leah reminded me," the man said.

"I had no choice." Leah's voice cut in. "I must protect the teachings of the Church, our mission, our existence. I must protect right from wrong, goodness from license. Let the sinners be consumed out of the earth, and let the wicked be no more. Psalms one hundred four; thirty-five."

"Don't mix steershit with salvation. Fargo, chapter one, verse one. Where'd you leave her?" he rasped.

"Not far from where we were camped. She was tied to a tree and gagged. I saw no reason for a scene. She was left food and water for when she frees herself, which she will do. We are not cruel."

"You're plumb loco, that's what you are," Fargo said.

"She will work herself loose of the bonds. She will make her way and have the chance to repent," Leah said.

"She'll have a chance to repent in a Shoshoni camp or facing a wolf pack," Fargo flung back. "And the worst thing about it is you really think you did right. You really believe you had to do this. *Goddamn!*"

"That is no way to use the Lord's name," Leah corrected sternly.

"It's better than twisting his message all the hell out of shape," Fargo said, spun on his heel, and started for the Ovaro.

"Where are you going?" Leah called.

"Where the hell do you think I'm going?" he threw back without turning.

"You can't. You're here to break trail for us. You have been paid to do that," Leah said.

He paused, looked back at her. "You better start praying, honey, because if I don't find her in one piece, this here mission of yours is at an end, and you with it," he said, and started to go on.

"Stop him!" He heard Leah give the order and saw Shadrach and Mishach step from behind one of the wagons to halt between him and the Ovaro.

"You heard Sister Leah," Mishach said.

"You've got three seconds to get out of my way or you're a dead disciple. Now you heard Brother Fargo." He counted off three seconds, started to move forward, and saw Mishach go for his gun. Whatever the man had once been, he hadn't been a gunfighter, Fargo realized as Mishach's draw was pitifully slow. Fargo's lightning movement had the big Colt out and firing in split seconds, and his shot blew the gun out of Mishach's hand before it had cleared the holster. Mishach cried out in pain and clutched his throbbing hand. By this time, Fargo had the big Colt shifted to point at Shadrach's chest. The man froze with his hand halfway to his holster, slowly dropped his arm to his side.

"Now, that's using a little common sense," Fargo said, and swung onto the pinto as Shadrach backed away.

Fargo sent the Ovaro into a full gallop and

headed back the way they had come. He grimaced as he rode, aware that they had been traveling the better part of the day. It'd be a long ride back even without being hindered by slow-moving wagons.

His thoughts turned to Leah as he rode, and he found himself frowning in wonder, unable to reconcile the smoldering, sensual creature and the misguided, sanctimonious tyrant. She led the others with her stern, unbending righteousness, and they were contentedly obedient, a cozy exchange of support and strength. Did she need the religious discipline because she was afraid of that throbbing sensuality inside her? he wondered. But that was too easy an explanation. She believed in her convictions. Twisted as they were, she believed in them. It was more likely that she'd never recognized the sensual part of her. You had to admit to something before you could be afraid of it, he thought with a tinge of bitterness. He hated the waste of anything beautiful. He was certain he'd hit home last night and that probably led her to this new twist of self-righteousness.

He felt the horse starting to shorten stride beneath him. He slowed at once, brought the horse down to a canter and then a walk. When the Ovaro had rested up, he resumed the pace, cursing the inexorable approach of dusk. But he had made good time and daylight still clung to the earth as he spotted the high lake and the place where they'd camped below it.

He raced to the site, turned the horse, and plunged into the trees to the south. He made a small half-circle and found nothing. He turned the horse west in the surrounding trees. He had almost completed another half-circle through the woodland when he reined to an abrupt halt as he saw

71

the young birch with the ropes lying at the base of it.

He dropped to the ground and swore softly as he picked up the ropes. She hadn't worked herself loose. The ropes had been cut. He scanned the ground and cursed again under his breath. The prints of Indian moccasins were clear in the forest floor. He'd been about an hour too late; the prints very fresh, the switchgrass under them still lying flat. They had gone on foot with her, three of them, he counted, and he led the Ovaro as he followed them in the fast-fading light.

They'd stayed in the woodlands, taken her to a place where they had left their ponies. He knelt down to examine the tracks again. Only three horses, he grunted as he swung onto the Ovaro. He followed, saw they had ridden casually, their ponies hardly digging into the grassy woodland soil. They'd put Rachel on one, it was obvious, and Fargo bent low in the saddle as he strained his eyes to follow the tracks as the dusk half-light began to dwindle away. He swore as night swallowed up the last of the dusk to leave the forest in blackness, the moon still too low to give much light.

He decided to take a calculated chance. The Indians had stayed in an absolutely straight line, and he continued on the same way, moving carefully through the trees. He drew in deep breaths as he let his nose take the place of his eyes. He'd gone on another quarter-mile or so through the woodland when he caught the sudden, musk-sharp smell of fish oil.

At the same instant he heard Rachel's voice, a sharp little cry, then an angry curse and another half-gasped cry, not more than two dozen yards ahead, he guessed. He swung from the Ovaro, pulled the horse along behind him as far as he dared, and left it beneath the wide low branches of a cottonwood. He went forward alone in a crouch, dropped to one knee as the woodland suddenly opened up. He saw a stream running downhill, the moonlight shining down on the cleared area bordering it.

The three Indians were there with Rachel. Shoshoni, he noted grimly. They had pulled clothes from her and were rolling her rounded nakedness in the stream, flipping her over, pulling her back. They were washing her off the way they'd wash off a piece of venison. As he watched, they pulled her from the stream.

One grabbed her from behind and lifted her up. The tallest of the trio, a wiry buck with stringy black hair held in place by a beaded brow band, yanked her up by the ankles so she was held in midair. He pulled her firm, young legs apart, and Fargo saw the panic on Rachel's round face as the rangy one, one hand on each leg, began to pull himself toward her. Fargo saw his loincloth start to rise and heard the Indian make little grunting sounds of anticipation. Rachel made a plaintive noise.

Fargo started to draw the Colt, but dropped it back into its holster. He didn't want shots that could bring others, and he reached down to his calf where the narrow calf holster circled his leg. He drew the thin, double-edged knife from its sheath and stepped forward, the distance still too far for accuracy in the dim light of the half-moon.

The Shoshoni spun at once, dropping Rachel, who hit the ground with a yelp. Fargo halted, met the tall, wiry buck's black eyes. He knew Shoshonean, the Comanche spoke it also.

"I come to talk," he said, and the tall buck took a step forward. Fargo pointed to Rachel, who had rolled to one side and was pulling on her skirt shirt. "Girl mine," he said.

The Northern Shoshoni, like most of the tribes, practiced communal property, but they respected the ownership of squaws. It was worth a try, Fargo figured. But the Indian shook his head. "She is gift," he said.

Fargo frowned. He saw Rachel on her feet, skirting around the other two bucks to come to his side.

"What's he saying?" she half-whispered.

"He says you're a gift," Fargo answered.

"How? They found me tied to the tree," Rachel said.

"Girl mine," Fargo said again to the Shoshoni.

"She gift from wagon people," the Indian said, his voice rising.

"Shit," Fargo muttered to Rachel. "They think you were a gift left by the others as a gesture. This is about as bad as it can be."

"Why?" Rachel asked.

"To take back a gift that has been accepted is as big an insult as you can give," Fargo explained.

The Shoshoni pointed to Rachel and struck his fist against his chest. The gift was his, and he had accepted for the Shoshoni, he was saying.

Fargo cursed silently. He had no choice but to carry through the insult. "I take back," he said, and emphasized the words with sign language gestures.

The rangy Indian whipped his tomahawk from the leather thong that circled his waist, and sprang into a crouch. Fargo stepped back, began to circle. The other two faded back. They would watch. It

74

was now a matter of honor between the one who had received the gift and the one who would take it back.

Fargo saw the rangy form move forward, shift to the right, and come in with a sideway swipe from the left. The tomahawk grazed the front of his shirt as he pulled back. He tried a quick counter and drove upward with the thin blade. But the Shoshoni was very fast. He ducked away from the thrust and brought the back of the tomahawk over and down. Fargo's fingers flew open with pain as the flat edge of the ax smashed into his wrist, and the knife dropped to the ground. He started to retrieve it, then flung himself to the side as the tomahawk whistled past his head to slam into the ground beside the knife.

Fargo hit the ground, rolled, came up on his feet, his wrist throbbing in pain. The Shoshoni came at him again, legs wide apart in a half-crouch, the tomahawk back in his hand. He feinted, but Fargo refused to be drawn in. The Indian feinted again, and once more Fargo wouldn't be baited. The Shoshoni seemed to try another feint, but Fargo knew he wouldn't try three in a row and he ducked low this time as the vicious swipe of the tomahawk passed over his head. He drove a straight left into the Indian's rangy midsection, all the power of his shoulders behind it. The blow landed deep into the buck's solar plexus, and he bent almost in half. The buck's eyes widened as the breath rushed from him. Fargo gritted his teeth for the pain he knew would come as he swung a roundhouse right. He connected with the Shoshoni's jaw, the pain searing through his wrist, but the Indian half-somersaulted backward and hit the ground hard.

Fargo rushed at him as the buck tried to rise, his

hand still clutching the short-handled ax as he fought for breath. He had gotten to his knees when Fargo's kick caught him in the side of the ribs. The Indian grunted in pain, and his breath again rushed from him as he fell and rolled half onto his back.

Fargo started for him, began his leap, and too late, saw the man flip the tomahawk in a short arc from where he lay on the ground. Fargo cursed silently as he tried to twist his body in midair, pull his head in, but the weapon hit him a glancing blow alongside the top of his head. Yellow and purple flashes went off in his head as he dropped to the ground. He tried to shake his head to clear it, but the multicolored lights still flashed inside him. He pulled himself to one knee, shook his head again and the lights stopped flashing. The ground swam into view just in time for him to see the Shoshoni's rangy form catapulting itself at him.

He pushed himself sideways as the Indian rushed toward him. The tall buck's momentum carried him past Fargo, and he hit the ground hard. Fargo rose, leapt for the Shoshoni as the man started to rise. The pain in his wrist shot through his forearm as he landed a looping right on the Indian's jaw, but the buck flew backward, landing inches from his tomahawk.

The Shoshoni seized the weapon, came up on his feet, and dived forward, his arm upraised to bring the ax down. Fargo held his position till the last fraction of a second, then dropped sideways just as the weapon was about to graze the side of his head. His shoulder slammed into the Indian's belly and the man grunted in pain as he fell forward, sprawled onto his face. Fargo leapt into the air and came down onto the Shoshoni's back with both feet.

He heard the snap of vertebrae as the buck screamed in anguish. Fargo stepped to the side as the Indian made a last feeble swipe with the tomahawk. He saw the buck try to roll over, then scream again in agony. Suddenly the Shoshoni's face grew dark and he gasped for breath. A long, terrible shudder ran through him and he lay still, the tomahawk falling from his hand.

Fargo looked at the two remaining Shoshoni, and his hand went to his gun. He'd have to use it if they came at him. He hadn't the strength to take them on now. But they silently turned away, pulled themselves onto their ponies, and rode along the edge of the stream, disappearing into the trees.

Fargo uttered a long sigh, walked to the stream, and immersed his wrist in the cool water as Rachel dropped to her knees beside him. "What now?" she asked.

"They'll go back and tell the others," Fargo said.

"Which means?"

"They probably would have attacked sometime, but now you can be damn sure they will," he said grimly. "They won't stand still for that insult. One thing more, they didn't just happen onto you. They saw you taken out there and left, and that means they're watching us." He drew his wrist from the water, the coolness easing the pain.

"I thought you'd find out too late to come back and help me," Rachel murmured.

"It damn near was too late," he said.

"How'd you find out I wasn't in the wagon?" she asked.

"I'll tell you while we ride. Let's get out of here,"

he said, and led her back to where the Ovaro waited. She sat in the saddle in front of him and leaned back against him as he told her what had happened at the riverbank.

"You think they've crossed on their own by now?" Rachel asked.

"I'd guess not. Leah will wait till morning to see if I get back. She won't risk the wagons if she can help it," Fargo said.

"That rotten bitch. I'll scratch her eyes out when I get back," Rachel said with a rush of anger.

"No," Fargo said sharply, and Rachel turned to frown at him. "You'll make it seem as though she was right about you," he said. "The others have already been turned against you. They'll be watching."

"What am I supposed to do?" Rachel protested.

"Nothing. Just come back, keep to yourself, and keep out of trouble," he said. "Stay in line. What's done is done. Leave it for now."

"Keeping to myself won't be hard," she grumbled.

"We'll be having enough trouble. I don't want any more," Fargo said as he pulled into a glen of hickory. "We'll rest a spell here," he said. "The horse is plumb tuckered out."

Rachel slid to the ground with him, and he unsaddled the pinto and laid the bedroll out. He undressed and stretched out. Rachel was beside him in moments, completely naked.

"Even tied to that tree I kept thinking about last night," she murmured.

"First tell me about the others. Start with Mishach and Shadrach. I know they've spent time on a chain gang," he said, and Rachel looked at him in surprise.

"Yes, for cattle rustling down Oklahoma way. Zeb and Ruth Classoon were in prison for swindling, Zach Kurtz for strangling his first wife. Eve Kurtz, though you'd never think it to look at her now, was a madam in a house where a sheriff was killed. They put her in jail for that."

"They're all ex-jailbirds?" Fargo frowned.

"Not the Spencers or the Tooners. They're just plain folk Reverend Johnston took into the Church. But Eb and Mary Carlton were part of a bank robbery that went wrong, and they served time for it."

"How come so many disciples are out of prison?" Fargo asked.

"Reverend Johnston preached in prisons all over. He used to say he wanted to help the sinners find God and the Church. I think he figured it was easier to convince those with no place else to turn, and as I said, he was a powerful preaching man. He brought them all into the Church when they left jail and made disciples out of all of them. Lord, they sure follow his teachings now," Rachel said.

"And Leah?" Fargo queried.

"Reverend Johnston raised her. He poured it all into her, especially about carrying on the Church. Listening to her is like listening to Reverend Johnston," Rachel said.

"One more question, maybe the most important," Fargo said. "What is this chosen place? Why is time so important in getting there?"

Rachel's hazel eyes were round with earnestness. "I don't know. I just know Reverend Johnston said they had to go there. That's why Leah calls it the chosen place, because he chose it. But I don't know why, and Pa never told me. But it has to have something to do with the Church, you can bet on it."

Fargo nodded in agreement, but the pressure of time still didn't fit it anyplace. He suspected that when he found out, he wouldn't be singing halle-lujah. He lay back, digesting the things Rachel had told him.

"That's all I know," Rachel said as her arms wrapped around him. She slid her body across his and cried out at the seasation, drew her curly little tangle across his organ. "Oh," she murmured, and her hands tightened against him. He felt himself responding instantly.

He pressed up against her, and her eyes grew wide, little gasps escaping from her. "Oh, yes," Rachel said, and once again her rounded, smooth, young body began to lift and pump. He tightened his hands around her waist, lifted her half into the air, and brought her down onto his rigidity and lowered her slowly. Then he let her go, and she plunged over him as she screamed in delight.

Staying inside her, he rolled over, and her firm young thighs locked around him. She cried out with little noises of pleasure, almost animallike sounds, as he drove deep, drew back, drove deeper still. Rachel was still not ready for the subtleties, and he had to wonder if she ever would be as she clasped him to her and vigorously pushed upward against his every thrust. She hurried pleasure, not with frantic haste but with a complete and thor-ough ecstasy in the wonders of her own body. She halted suddenly, arched her back, and pulled his face down to her breasts as she came to her climax with a deep sigh full of fulfillment and regret at the same time.

She lay against him later, holding him tight, and

slept in satisfied exhaustion. He slept until the first gray light of dawn stole through the trees. He came awake and shook her. She opened her eyes, looking sleepily edible. But he pushed away from her and dressed, then shook her again. She stood up and began to don clothes.

"We've riding to do," he said as he saddled the Ovaro, letting her use his canteen to freshen up. He swung her up onto the horse with him.

"I don't know how long I can be good when we get back," she said.

"Work on it," he growled. "That's an order."

She nodded and leaned hard against him as they rode. He put the pinto into a fast canter. When they came in sight of the riverbank, the wagons were still lined up there. The morning prayer service circle was in session, and it came to an end as he rode up, halted, and slid from the saddle with Rachel. Everyone watched as she walked, head held high, to her wagon. Preacher Thomas detached himself from the others and hurried after her to the wagon.

Fargo met Leah as she came toward him. Her face showed only a formal stiffness but the sensual loveliness was still in her smoldering gray-blue eyes and full lower lip. Two people in one, he murmured to himself. "We must talk, Fargo," she said.

"We should get these wagons across," he answered.

She met his hard stare and nodded. "We'll talk later," Leah said.

"Whenever," he muttered, and turned to see Mishach studying him, the others behind him near the riverbank.

"You are very fast with your gun, Fargo," the man said. "I must remember that."

"Just remember I don't take to being bothered," Fargo returned and the man turned away, a strange smile on his face. Fargo turned to Leah and the others. "Nothing's changed. Only the driver crosses with the wagon," he said. "Every wagon across will make the bottom clay softer, so the heaviest wagons go first." His eyes went to the Carltons' big California rack-bed rig. "That means you first," he said, and Eb Carlton climbed aboard the big wagon and lifted the reins.

"Make a wide circle here and hit the water going full out," Fargo said, and watched as the man obeyed, snapping his whip over the team. The horses surged forward, sprayed water high as they plunged into the shallow grayish river.

Fargo watched with tight lips as the big wagon began to slow mid-river, the wheels sinking below the water. But Eb Carlton used his whip again, and the horses pulled harder and brought their burden onto the opposite bank.

"The two Conestogas next, one at time," Fargo said. "Same thing, hit the water going full out."

The Spencers moved first and again his eyes followed the wagon as it plunged into the water and made it across to the other bank. Paul Tooner sent his wagon racing into the water next, but the second Conestoga markedly slowed when it reached mid-river, and Fargo saw the horses pulling hard, bringing their legs up high as they pulled free of the soft clay bottom.

"Use your whip, dammit," he shouted, and Paul Tooner yanked the whip from its rack, snapped it across the rumps of both horses. With a snort of protest, the horses dug in harder, pulled, and the big Conestoga slowly continued rolling on, picking up speed as it reached the firmer underfooting of the bank.

"No more crossings here," Fargo said to the others as the second Conestoga rolled from the river. "Move down a dozen yards," he said, and led the way to another place. He sent Zeb Classoon over with his Owensboro followed by Zach Kurtz. Rachel met his glance as he sent Preacher Thomas over next, and lastly Leah in her light converted milk wagon. She crossed without trouble.

"I'll take you over," he said to Rachel as Shadrach and Mishach started to ferry the other women across. "You and your pa talk it out?" he asked as the Ovaro moved into the water.

"I wouldn't exactly call it that. We had a few words," Rachel said.

"Such as?" Fargo asked.

"He said my being saved was a sign of the Lord's forgiveness."

"I'm afraid to ask, but what did you say?" Fargo queried.

"I said it was a sign of his approval." She giggled. "He about fell out of the wagon."

Fargo laughed quietly. She was a little hellcat. "I still want you to stay low, keep away from starting trouble."

"I will—for you," she murmured, and he was satisfied she meant it.

He let her down on the far bank and rode back to take part in the task of bringing over the trunks and other heavy possessions. The entire operation took more time than he'd expected, and when the wagons were finally reloaded and ready to roll, the sun had gone into the midday sky. He gestured to the trail, which continued this side of the gray-white river and rode on into the next hill.

Once again, his eyes scanned the tops of the ridges as he rode, and he caught a glimpse of a lone near-naked horseman filtering through the high timber. There were others, he knew. He didn't need to see them. Right now they were still content to watch and wait. But he knew that time would end in a blaze of hate and revenge.

He rode on, and as night neared, he found a place in the shade of a line of shadbush. He had the Ovaro unsaddled and fed before the wagons rolled in. Supper was prepared quietly by the women and he noted that Rachel sat beside her pa as she ate in silence. The meal ended quickly, and the others had begun to file into their wagons when he saw Leah approach. He pushed himself to his feet.

She halted in front of him and the deep blue eyes searched his face. "The spirit of forgiveness was not with me this morning," she said. "Perhaps it would have been better than punishment."

"The high priestess admits she can be wrong? That's a step in the right direction," Fargo said.

She ignored the sarcasm in his voice, and her earnest expression never changed. "Your actions showed me that forgiveness was the better way," Leah said.

"You have the damnedest way of twisting things all wrong," Fargo said. "I went back for Rachel because you'd no damn right leaving her there. Forgiveness hadn't a damn thing to do with it."

"Nevertheless, you showed me that I perhaps was wrong," Leah said.

"No damn perhaps in it," Fargo insisted.

"That's unimportant now," Leah said, refusing

to concede the point. "What matters is that your actions lost us more than half a day of valuable time. That must not happen again."

"That's up to you, honey," Fargo said.

Leah stepped closer. "You do believe in good Church teachings. I have seen that. I know you can draw closer to the Church. Listen to your soul," she said.

"Listen to your body," he replied.

"I will reach you, Fargo," Leah said firmly.

"Keep trying. You might come up with something." He grinned.

"The work of the Church and this mission comes before everything else. Nothing must interfere with that," Leah reaffirmed.

"I hear you honey." Fargo nodded.

Leah searched his face for another moment, then turned and strode to her wagon as he enjoyed the smooth sway of her hips.

He set his bedroll out at the far end of the camp and slept soundly through the night to wake with the new day's sun. Morning prayer service was still going on as he rode from camp and headed up the remainder of the hill until he reached the crest. He halted there to gaze appreciatively ahead.

The land dipped down and beyond it, the red, yellow, and deep burnt-orange of great faces of stone were lighted brilliantly by the sun as the painted hills rose up in all their majesty. He saw the sun-speckled blue Deschutes River beyond, where it threaded its way through the center of the Cascade Range. He hurried down, cantered to the river, and waited till the wagons came into sight. He motioned to a wide swatch of a path that ran alongside the river, and set out again.

The path paralelled the Deschutes in an uneven

fashion, weaving in and out of the low hills as the colorful great stone faces reflected the sun. Their rugged beauty held a hundred hiding places, he knew, and his eyes swept their uneven crags and crevices. He'd ridden for almost another hour when he spotted the two Shoshoni across the river as they rode along a ledge in the painted cliffs. They vanished into a deep crevice and he rode on until the day began to wear down. He found a place not far from the river to make camp, then dismounted and relaxed till the wagons rolled up in the dusk.

Supper was taken again in almost total silence, and he noticed Rachel stay beside her pa during the meal. She hurried into her wagon when she finished, her face glowering, and he smiled to himself. She was obeying his orders, and not at all happy about it.

He took his bedroll, walked to a spot near the riverbank, where a thicket of dwarf maple afforded a screen of privacy. He spread his things out at the far side of the thicket, had just sat down to pull off boots when he heard someone approaching. He rose as he glimpsed the deep-blond hair through the low trees, and waited as Leah halted before him.

"I saw you go this way and thought I'd find you here," she said. "I came to tell you I think it's time you attended morning prayer service, Fargo," she said. "All the followers resent your staying away."

"I'm all upset about that," Fargo said.

"It is a sin to turn away from the Word," Leah said.

"Joy to the world, remember. That's the word, honey. You haven't got it. We went through this. I still haven't seen a smile," Fargo told her.

"You will when we reach the chosen place and complete our mission," Leah said.

"No sale. Wrong kind of smile, wrong kind of job," he answered.

"You are a man of great stubbornness, Fargo," Leah said with grudging approval. "Good night."

He tossed her a quick smile, and she walked back into the night. He waited and suddenly smiled. His wildcat's hearing told him she had stopped in the dark of the trees. He smiled to himself as he began to undress, slowly peeling off his shirt, then trousers. When he had stripped almost naked, he stretched his powerful, magnificently proportioned body under the pale light of the half-moon. He lay down, stretched out, and smiled again as he picked up the faint rustle of leaves. Leah was hurrying away, and he grunted wryly. The cloak of righteous purity was slipping. Would it slip far enough before the Shoshoni attacked? The hope was laced with the dark foreshadowing of the redman's fury. He turned on his side and let sleep sweep over him.

Morning sent him to campsite as the prayer service was ending. He saddled up the Ovaro, and watched Rachel pass by on her way to the Owensboro seed-bed rig. She glanced at him furtively. Her lips held a pout and her eyes a plea. "You're doing real well," he said to her.

She muttered as she strode on. He laughed softly, swung onto the Ovaro, and paused as he saw Shadrach, Mishach, and Zach Kurtz watching.

"Keeping tabs?" Fargo slid out calmly.

Mishach's mouth seemed to take on more lines of severity. "Sister Leah has said she does not want another occasion of sin," he rasped.

"Not for Rachel, anyway," Fargo said, and smiled at the frowns of consternation that crossed their faces. He wheeled the horse around and rode away at a fast trot, sending the pinto along the path that roughly paralelled the river. The path rose gently, moved higher opposite the sun-painted hills, and he again glimpsed the horseman high atop the rocks. They were letting him see an ocassional observer and yet they still held back. They must have had a reason, but he didn't want to think about it yet. There was nothing to be gained by hurrying the inevitable.

He speeded the pinto's pace, followed a dip in the path, and suddenly reined up as the river curved in front of him. The curve forked in three places, and he felt the excitement catch at him. He dismounted and waited, and Leah's wagon rolled up first. She almost leapt from the driver's seat and ran to stand at the edge of the river, where it branched off into three small tributaries.

"You have found it," she cried out. "Now we go north to find the hill with an altar of stone." She whirled and touched his arm. She exuded an excitement he'd never seen in her before. Her eyes were shining; in fact, they glistened with more than enthusiastic excitement, he shrewdly noted. A strange, fervid light filled the usually smoldering orbs, and she pressed his arm again. "We must hurry even faster, now," Leah said.

"To find more signs at the chosen place," he said sarcastically, and the shining light left her eyes at once to be replaced by the familiar cautious veil.

"Yes," she said. Leah was evading again. She became more and more of a fascinating enigma, and a feeling of urgency suddenly swept over him, a dark feeling that told him he was involved with forces that presaged disaster. He looked beyond the deep-blond cascade of hair. Directly north led into the heart of the Painted Hills with their rocks and crags and stands of scraggly brush, red cedar, balsam, and lodgepole pine. He pointed to a trail that narrowed but stayed wide enough for a single lane of wagons.

"Follow that. I'll ride ahead," he told her, and sent the pinto on just as the other wagons began to roll into sight. He took the trail that rose gently then plunged deep into the hills. He rode with cautious haste through sides of flat rock and twisting crags with dozens of narrow openings and balsam that grew in clusters. A brief flash higher in the hills caught his eye, and he glanced up to see the Indian disappear behind a crag. The sun had caught the polished surface of an elk's-tooth pendant for an instant, and Fargo's lips grew tight.

The Shoshoni continued his watch, and Fargo knew that each watchful moment only ensured the inevitable attack. It was becoming plain that they were curious about where the wagons were headed and had decided to wait and see. But more important, they were content to let the intruders venture deeper and deeper into their heartland until there'd be no escape. Fargo decided to finish the job, find the chosen place for Leah, and then hightail out of there while he still had his scalp.

He crested a rise in the narrow trail, went down the other side into a valleylike dip of land, and rode through it as the day began to near an end. He pulled under a line of balsams for the night, unsaddled his pinto, and was relaxed when the wagons arrived. Leah and Preacher Thomas conferred in low, earnest tones during supper, and he watched Rachel eat alone beside her wagon. He was tempted to sit with her but decided against it. He went to sleep early, anxious for the new day to arrive.

He was up and ready when it did, and he rode from camp as the others were preparing for morning prayer service. Hugging the side of the trail where it narrowed, he spotted a passage that went up into the hills in a steep incline, and left the trail to climb up the twisting path. He halted where it leveled off, and surveyed the terrain ahead. He saw nothing that resembled a stone altar, so he made his way back down to the trail. He rode on, and the trail grew narrow again, became twisting as it narrowed, but the wagons could negotiate the turns, he decided, and cantered on. He had just rounded another turn when he saw before him two Shoshoni on ponies, between twin, thick stands of red cedar flanking both sides of the road.

Fargo's hand went to the big Colt at his hip as he reined to a halt. He recognized the two that had been there when he'd taken Rachel back. They sat their ponies silently, unmoving, and their black eyes bored into him for a long moment until silently they turned, and faded into the thick stands of cedar, one into one side, the other into the opposite. Fargo cursed under his breath and sent the Ovaro on. They had been sent down as a reminder. And a promise, he grunted grimly. He galloped past the red cedars and continued on along the passageway, which straightened and began to dip.

The first purple veil of dusk began to spread along the edge of the sky as the trail opened into a flat hollow of land. He glimpsed a small hill at one end of the hollow, a house atop it, but it was the construction of rocks at the base of the hill that held his gaze. He reined to a halt as he stared at the pieces of stone transformed by wind, weather, and ancient land movement into a monolithic sculpture.

Two short, thick pieces of stone supported each end of a long, flat slab that looked remarkably like the smooth, flat top of an altar. Atop one end of the slab of stone, a dishlike piece of stone rested, and at the other end a tall, thin, twisting formation rose up as though it were a giant stone candle. "The altar of stone," Fargo murmured. It existed, he saw not without a sense of awe, far larger than any man-made altar, yet unmistakably similar.

He dismounted, walked to the great stone altar, and circled it. His eyes scanned the nearby hill and the house atop it.

A small spiral of smoke came from the chimney. The house itself was a strange little structure made of logs, a frame window set in the center, a high, peaked roof, and a short chimney. It sat on the flat part of the hill, looking not unlike a doll's house that had been set on a table. He heard the creak of wagon wheels, turned, and watched the caravan roll into the hollow of land, Leah's converted green milk wagon in the lead.

She halted at once and leapt from the wagon. Fargo watched the others pull up next to her and behind. They quickly formed a circle and moved slowly toward the stone altar.

Fargo walked to Leah. The burning, fervid light shone in her deep-blue eyes again. "It is the place," she said to him. "The chosen place that was described to Reverend Johnston."

"He had some kind of dream?" Fargo inquired.

"More than a dream. The Lord has blessed us with a quest to follow," Leah said.

"What now?" Fargo asked.

"There will be other signs," she said firmly. "We will camp there at the base of the hill." She gestured to a spot where a half-dozen dwarf maples formed a semicircle. Fargo's glance swept the little hollow in the fading light. The low, flat-topped hill formed part of the hollow, taking up the north end of it, but beyond the little hill the hollow was surrounded by tall slopes of rock and timber. All in all, it was a very vulnerable spot.

Fargo grimaced and fixed Leah with a hard stare as the others began to move their wagons down to the base of the hill. "You figure to stay here long?" he asked.

"That depends," she answered as Preacher Thomas came up to them.

"I'd suggest you camp someplace else," Fargo said.

"Oh, no," both Leah and Preacher Thomas said almost in unison. "We must stay here—for now, at least," Leah added.

Fargo's glance went to the little house on top of the hill. "Because somebody else beat you to the chosen spot?" he asked.

"No, because we must search for the signs yet to be revealed to us," Leah said firmly. "We'll talk more later," she added as she strode to her wagon.

Fargo led the pinto down after her to the trees she had chosen as a campsite.

She came to him later as the others made fires for supper. She followed as he stared up the hill to the house, where a pinpoint of light flickered from the window. "I should like to know who lives there," she said.

"Kind of curious, myself," he admitted.

"Would you go see?" Leah asked, and he paused before answering. Something in her voice, a controlled casualness, belied her very active interest and made him wonder if it was simple curiosity or something more. His eyes moved to her and slowly traveled up and down the full-breasted, sensual figure.

"I'll think about it," he said.

Leah stepped closer, and he smelled the faint musky womanly odor of her. "Please do," she said. "You have done well, Fargo. It is a sign you should be one of us."

"I'll think about that, too," he said.

"I hope so," Leah said, and gazed up at him with eyes full of earnestness. "Enjoy supper. There are things I must discuss with Preacher Thomas and some of the others. I will look for you in the morning," she said.

He watched her cross the campsite. Supper was served soon after as darkness closed in, and he saw Leah in an earnest conversation with Preacher Thomas, Shadrach, Mishach, and Zach Kurtz. He strolled past Rachel as he returned his tin plate.

She glowered at him. "I can't keep this up much longer," she muttered. "Being cooped up inside that wagon is getting me crazy."

"You've done real well. Maybe now that we're here, things will change," Fargo said.

"Don't bet on it," Rachel said bitterly.

"Hang in there," he told her as he went on and sat down against a tree trunk.

Leah ended her conference and the others drifted to their wagons as the moon began to climb into the night sky.

Fargo peered across the dark to the little house

atop the hill as his curiosity grew. There was only one way to satisfy it, he muttered to himself as he rose to his feet, climbed onto the Ovaro, and moved from the campsite. He rode slowly up the low hill to the house, where firelight still flickered from inside. He couldn't imagine anyone living out here except maybe a mountain man with a squaw wife, or a hermit. Neither would be the kind to welcome visitors, he knew. He cantered loudly straight to the front door so he'd be both seen and heard. He had neared the front door when a voice called out sharply.

"That's far enough," it said, and he frowned as he pulled to a halt. The door opened and the figure in the doorway held a rifle trained on his chest. The light from inside the house revealed a young woman in a skirt and checkered shirt. He took in a face all angles and planes, a thin nose and a wide mouth, dark eyebrows and dark-brown hair held in place with a red ribbon. He couldn't make out the color of her eyes, but it was an attractive face, strong without being hard. Beneath it, a long neck curved into a lean, neat body, smallish breasts under the checkered shirt, and a tight, trim figure.

"I told you not to come around here again, and I meant it," she said. "I'll put a bullet in you."

"Hold on, honey. You didn't tell me anything," Fargo said.

"I told the big one with the mustache," she said. "Now get out of here before I start shooting."

"You've got something all wrong. I'm not with any big man with a mustache," Fargo said.

She peered down the rifle barrel at him. "Move over into the light," she said. "Nice and easy."

Fargo dismounted slowly and stepped into the

shaft of yellow light from the doorway, and he saw her frown as she looked him over.

"You haven't been around before, but that doesn't mean you're not one of them," she muttered.

"One of who?" Fargo asked.

"The three roustabouts that have been after me," she snapped.

"I'm with those wagons below, broke trail for them to get here. Name's Fargo . . . Skye Fargo," he said.

He watched her consider his words. "Why'd you come up here?" she queried.

"Curious," he said.

"If you're with the wagons, you'll be moving on, come morning," she said.

"No, they're figuring to stay here a spell. They're missionary folk."

"I don't need any sermons," she said tartly. "I want quiet and peace. Why are they going to stay here?"

"They say it's a chosen place," Fargo told her.

She looked annoyed. "Seems by too many people," she said. "Tell them not to bother me, if you're really with them."

"I told you I was." He frowned.

"You can tell me Abe Lincoln sent you. That doesn't make it so. You could still be with those other three," she returned.

"Maybe there are no other three. Maybe you're just a crazy woman living out here alone," Fargo snapped back.

"You can get out of here, mister," she said, and raised the rifle.

He shrugged, took the Ovaro by the reins, and started to walk down the hillside. He was halfway down the slope when he heard her voice call after him.

"I'm no crazy woman. They camp south of the first ridge," she said, and he looked up in time to see her stalk into the little house and slam the door shut.

He reached the bottom of the hill, still frowning. His curiosity hadn't grown any less. She'd been a surprise, that was for sure. Why was she out here alone in this isolated, Shoshoni held territory? His glance went to the campsite. It was still, a sleeping place. And why had Leah rushed to this chosen place? There were unanswered questions all over. But perhaps he could get one answer, he murmured to himself, swung onto the pinto, and set off south.

The moon touched the ridge as he rode up across a low ridge and spotted the flicker of a campfire beyond the cedars. He walked the horse forward and came to a halt in the trees a dozen yards from where three men sat around a dying fire. The nearest one was tall, long legs stretched out toward the fire. He had black, stringy long hair, and a dyspeptic face, as though he were constantly tasting something sour. The second man sat cross-legged, and his hands twitched, brushed his shirt, rubbed his trouser legs, never stopping their nervous little motions. He had a sallow complexion that made him look as though he had skin of wax. The third one wore no hat and was mostly bald, with little tufts of reddish hair clustered around the top of his ears. He had a small-eyed face with meanness hanging in every feature, a thick mustache under a flat nose. They were all middle-aged, he guessed.

Fargo's lips pursed in thought as he peered at

the trio. The girl in the little house had told him the truth about them. They existed, and it seemed they had some reason to go after her. Something more than just horniness, he was certain, going by the feeling inside him that he had long learned never to discount.

He quietly turned the Ovaro and headed back into the little hollow. The girl in the house continued to dance in his thoughts. She was still a mystery living all alone out here, and perhaps the three men weren't the only ones with more than a passing interest in her, he reflected as he thought of how Leah's question had seemed all too casual.

He reached the hollow, and saw the little house atop the hill was dark. He tethered the Ovaro at the campsite, took his bedroll a dozen yards away, and undressed to his B.V.D.s in the warm night. He lay awake for a little while as thoughts rolled around inside his head like so many tumbleweeds. He never liked unfinished tasks. He'd nail down a few answers before he went his way.

He didn't like being taken in, either, and Leah had constantly evaded any real answers about this chosen place. He embraced sleep with a kind of grim decision.

5

When morning came, Fargo stayed where he had slept, his gear rolled up beside him. He watched the morning prayer service through the trees and frowned as the circle broke up. Only Rachel hurried to her wagon this time. The others, in small groups of two and three, began to walk toward the stone altar, and Fargo rose to his feet, stepped closer through the trees to watch. They reached the altar, all except Leah, who waited by her wagon, and Fargo saw them move around the big stones, examine them at all sides. They walked back and forth around the structure, then crossed and recrossed the land around it.

They walked slowly, paused often to stare at the ground, and went on as they made a zigzag pattern from the big stones back to the campsite. Fargo watched, his eyes narrowed, and saw the group go through the campsite and move out beyond it. They almost crossed to the edge of the hollow and then back again. Every step was taken slowly, heads bowed, crossing and recrossing the ground with the same, deliberate zigzag pattern until they all returned to the campsite again. This time they went into their wagons to disappear inside, and Fargo pushed the frown from his brow. He glanced up to the sun. To his surprise, the orange sphere had begun to cross into the afternoon sky. He'd been so fascinated watching them that he hadn't been aware of how long it had taken. He picked up his bedroll and strode to the wagons.

He put his gear onto the Ovaro and halted at the converted milk wagon. Leah opened the sliding side door, and he stepped inside without waiting for an invitation. His quick glance took in the cot along one side of the interior, the trunk at the other, and two large pillows of cotton ticking forming seats in the back corner. Leah's eyes held a tiny frown as she met his gaze.

He chose words carefully. "Maybe you'd like to tell me what that was all about?" he slid at her.

"A ceremony," she said smoothly. "We walk the earth in a ritual of celebration for having arrived here."

"It seemed more search than celebration," Fargo remarked.

Leah half-shrugged. "Perhaps it seemed that way to you," she said. "However, it is ritual." She met his gaze with unwavering firmness. She could lie as well as she could evade in the name of the Church, he decided. "I wondered where you were," she said. "I thought perhaps you'd gone to see about the house on the hill."

"Did that last night," he said casually, and saw the flare of instant interest that touched her face.

"Who's living there?" Leah asked, and he saw the effort she put into making the question appear casual.

"A girl," he said, and the flare of excitement grew in the smoldering blue eyes.

"A girl? Alone out here? That's unusual, to say the least," Leah answered with controlled carefulness.

"It is," he agreed blandly as he decided to draw her out and see how much she'd reveal.

"She say anything about herself?" Leah asked.

"Not much," Fargo answered, and saw impatience touch Leah's face.

Her full, sensual lips tightened, but she kept her voice even. "I think you should find out more," Leah said.

"Maybe," Fargo remarked. "I might pay another visit."

"I wish you would, Fargo," Leah said, tried to sound merely curious, and failed.

"Those new signs show themselves yet?" Fargo queried.

"No," she said, "except perhaps for you." His brows lifted. "Yes, you, Fargo," Leah said. "You are a sign. Your wisdom in finding the trail here for us. It is all a sign you should be one of us." She stepped forward, cupped both hands around his face, a warm, gentle pressure. She closed her eyes as she held his head in her hands. "Don't you feel the spirit flowing from my touch?" she said breathlessly.

One round breast curved hard against her blouse to pull it tight, the faintest tiny bulge in the center of the fabric only an inch from his face. "I sure feel something," he agreed.

Leah's eyes stayed close and her hands continued to cup his face. "It is the spirit," she murmured, and he nodded. She had to put a spiritual face on the feelings that were stirring inside her, he decided. It didn't bother him any. They were stirring and that's what counted. He moved and brushed against the full breast so close to him. Leah's eyes snapped open, and she drew her hands away. He saw the faint flush tinge her cheeks, but she gathered herself at once.

"Tell me what you found out about the girl," she said firmly.

He let the edge come into his voice. "Tell me why this is the chosen place?" he countered.

Leah hesitated, and he saw her lips tighten. "When you are one of us, I can tell you everything," she said. Maybe she meant it, Fargo wondered, and maybe it was but another turn-aside answer. Either way, she was going to learn he could play her game and win.

"Keep trying," he told her, slid the door open, and swung down from the wagon. He caught the little frown of thought on her face as she pulled the door closed. He mounted the Ovaro and slowly moved from the campsite as his eyes swept the hollow of land.

The small hill with the house atop it lay not quite at the center of the hollow, and the land stayed flat around the base of it until it reached the tall stone and timber hills that surrounded it on all sides. He sent the Ovaro to the closest of the hills around the hollow and rode up onto the slope. He scouted the terrain thoroughly and moved onto the hills that bordered the north end of the hollow. He did the same there, then moved on into the hills at the west edge of the hollow. Again he rode slowly, painstakingly canvassing the terrain of timber and stone, and went on to the south edge of the hollow.

Night had begun to lower over the land when he finished scouting the south hills. He halted at their base to dismount and stretched himself over a soft bed of nut moss. He had scouted thoroughly, seen the Indian pony prints that marked every side of the hollow, pursued the trails and creviced passages that were woven through each section. If he were a Shoshoni chief, he could ask for no better place from which to mount an attack. Plenty of recessed passages let an attacker come close unseen and afforded the opportunity to swoop down from all four sides.

The chosen place was a damn trap, but he knew it'd be all but impossible to convince Leah to move on. He pushed himself to his feet and swung onto the Ovaro. Maybe a visit to the three men might provide some answers. The girl claimed they were after her, and she certainly had been on guard. Besides, they weren't the type to be hiding behind any missionary curtain. It was worth a try.

He sent the Ovaro up over the south ridge and down the other side and saw the flicker of a campfire where he had found it the night before. At least they stayed in one place, he thought. But only two figures came into sight as he neared, both huddled around the small fire. He halted in the trees, waited, his eyes scouring the nearby darkness while his ears probed the stillness. The third man was missing. Fargo frowned. He strained his ears for the sound of someone gathering firewood, but only the howl of a distant wolf came to him. The frown dug deeper into his brow as he wheeled the Ovaro and started back toward the hollow. He walked the horse until he was far enough from the campfire and then put the pinto into a full gallop. The missing member of the trio wasn't anywhere nearby, and the nearest town to get a drink was a hundred miles away. The girl's words hung in his mind as he raced over the low ridge and down into the hollow, heading the pinto to the back side of the small hill. He kept the horse at a full gallop until he was almost to the top of the hill, and reined in as the house appeared in front of him. He heard the girl's voice, a sharp cry of pain and anger, and he swung from the saddle and started for the house in a low crouch.

The front door was ajar, lamplight streaming into the night. He reached the doorway and edged closer to peer inside. He saw the girl on the floor, her wrists tied together as the man rolled her onto her back directly in front of the fireplace. It was the bald-headed one with the small-eyed, mean face and the big reddish mustache, Fargo saw. The man drew a red-hot poker from the fireplace and brandished it over the girl. "I'm tired of waiting around. You talk or I'll brand you in so many places you'll never go outside again," he snarled.

"I don't know anything. God, why can't you believe me?" the girl said.

"Because you're lying, you little bitch," the man shouted.

Fargo unholstered the big Colt and stepped into the room. "Drop the poker, mister," he growled, and saw the man's head spin around, surprise in his face.

"Who the hell are you?" The man frowned.

"Her fairy godmother. Drop the poker," Fargo said.

The man's mean face grew meaner as the corners of his mouth turned down. "I'll drop it, right on her face," the man rasped, and moved the red-hot poker directly over her cheek. He flicked a glance at the big man with the gun. "Drop the Colt or she's going to look like a side of Texas steer."

Fargo swore under his breath. He could take the man out with one shot but the sizzling poker would still fall onto the girl's face. Slowly, he lowered his hand, opened his fingers, and let the gun drop to the floor. "Now put down the poker," he said.

"Kick the gun over here," the man said.

Fargo kicked the gun, sending it spinning against the far wall.

"Son of a bitch," the man muttered as he watched the gun go into the wall.

Fargo leapt forward, and the man's eyes snapped back to him. He spun, swinging the red-hot poker exactly as Fargo had expected. He dropped almost to his hands and knees and felt the heat of the poker as it grazed the top of his head. He came up with his left, caught the man behind the elbow, and seized his wrist with his right hand. He twisted up and down at the same time, and the man yelled out in pain as the poker fell from his hand.

Fargo spun him around, brought up a sharp, short right that caught the man under the jaw. The man half-flew backward, falling only a few feet from the door. Fargo crossed the room in three long strides, scooped up the Colt, and spun around to see the man half-rolling, half-diving out the door. He started after the fleeing figure as the man raced around the side of the house and leapt onto a brown horse. Fargo raised the Colt as the man started to gallop away, but let his arm go to his side, and the man fled safely down the back side of the hill. He waited until the sound of the galloping horse faded away, then turned back into the house. The girl had pushed herself to a sitting position, and Fargo knelt down and untied her wrist ropes.

She had brown eyes, he saw at last, and close up, her face was softer, the planes and angles less pronounced than they'd been in the shadows.

"He must have been waiting outside," she said as she rubbed her wrists. "I stepped out to throw away some slops, and he tackled me." Her eyes took in Fargo's handsome, chiseled strength with appreciative eyes. "I owe you an apology as well as a lot of thanks."

"You can tell me what this is all about," Fargo said. "Start with yourself."

"I'm Diane Keller," she said as she stood up and smoothed her skirt and blouse. He saw that the smallish breasts were beautifully matched to her trim, lean figure. She reached behind the outer stones of the fireplace and brought out an earthen jug and two clay cups. "I could stand a drink, and you look like a man who seldom refuses one," she said.

"Close enough." He laughed as she poured and handed him one of the clay cups. He took a draw of the liquid and found it good, rich, aged rye whiskey. Diane sat down cross-legged on the floor opposite him and he caught a glimpse of her lean, strong legs. "Why are those men after you, Diane Keller?" he asked.

"They think I know where twenty thousand dollars is hidden," she said, and Fargo let out a low whistle.

"That's a lot of money. Men have killed for a lot less than that," he said. "Why do they think you know where it is?"

"They think my father told me. He's the one who hid it away," she answered.

"Did he?" Fargo asked.

"No, he never mentioned it to me. I don't know a damn thing about the money, only they don't believe me," Diane said. "When they first came, they asked where the money was, even offered to give me a piece of it. Then they demanded I tell them, and finally they started threatening me."

"Do you know anything about the money, where it was from?" Fargo queried.

"No, and when I asked them that, they told me not to take them for fools. They just won't believe I'm not lying," Diane said. Her brown eyes were dark with sincerity, and he'd picked up no glibness in her answers, yet there was something that nudged at him.

"Why are you out here in this wild place alone?" he asked. "How'd you know about this house out here?"

Her lips formed a rueful little smile. "You're wondering if I really came out here to hide away," she said.

"The thought occurred to me," he admitted.

She rose abruptly, went to a corner of the house, and returned with a large artist's sketch pad filled with loose sheets of paper. She sat down beside him, opened it, and put it on his lap. He looked down at the first sheet where, a lovely drawing of a stiff-leafed aster filled the page. She turned the page, and he saw a drawing of a swamp buttercup.

"Go on, look through them yourself," she said, and he turned the big sheets to see drawing upon drawing, many in color, of wildflowers. She had captured wild indigo, devil's paintbrush, bellwort, Indian cucumber, Saint-John's-wort, orange milkweed, spotted jewelweed, fringed loosestrife, and a host of others. He closed the pages of the big pad and met her gaze.

"I'm doing a book of wildflowers for a publisher back East," she said. "As for the house, my father brought me here. He had it built years back."

Fargo frowned at her. "Then maybe the money

106

does exist," he said. "Maybe those three are right about that."

"Maybe it does, but that puts me in the same place. I don't know about it," Diane answered. "I was only nine when my father left. I didn't see him again until a little over a year ago when he suddenly showed up. It seems he'd always kept track of where I'd lived with my mother until she died."

"What happened after he suddenly showed up?" Fargo asked.

"He moved in with me. He told me he was sick, with not a long time to live, and he wanted to spend the last of his life with his daughter. It was a new thing, getting to know him again, fun in its own way," Diane said as she thought back, a tiny smile touching her face. "He was really very nice, as nice as I'd remembered him. When he found out I was doing a book on wildflowers, he brought me here. I was excited. I had practically every wildflower there is in my backyard, so to speak. He died suddenly soon after, and I came back here to do the book by myself."

"He tell you anything about the years you'd never seen him or heard from him?" Fargo questioned.

"No, that was a closed chapter of his life, he said," Diane replied.

"How do you manage to stay here in the middle of Northern Shoshoni country and keep alive?" Fargo asked.

"When I first got here, I helped a young Shoshoni girl who'd been hurt in a fall. They've left me alone ever since. Their way of repaying me, I suppose," Diane said, and Fargo nodded agreement. "It's really ironic, the Indians leave me alone, and these three bastards won't," she added.

Fargo found himself believing Diane Keller. She had a rough-edged honesty about her, and she'd answered his questions openly. He was convinced she didn't know if or why or where the money was hidden. He pushed himself to his feet and extended a hand. She took it, and the smallish breasts bounced saucily under the checkered shirt as she sprang up.

"Maybe I can find some answers for both of us," Fargo said.

"From those three? How?" Diane frowned.

"They want that money. They'll talk if they think maybe I can help them," he said.

"Will you come back?" she asked.

"When I've something to tell you," he said.

"No need to wait for that. You've earned a welcome here anytime," she said. "And I still owe you. Besides, I've questions to ask you."

"I'll come back," he said as she went outside with him. Her eyes lighted with an artist's appreciation of beauty as she saw the Ovaro.

"How magnificent," she murmured. She turned to him and reached up, and Fargo felt her lips brush his cheek. "You, too," she said, and half-ran back to the house.

He chuckled as he swung onto the horse and rode south. He headed toward the flickering campfire in the distance and reflected that nothing he had learned explained Leah's more-than-casual interest in Diane Keller. Maybe the three men taking shape around the fire could answer that, he grunted as he neared them, reined up, and slid from the horse. He drew the big Sharps from its saddle holster and began to push through the cedars. The men's voices came to him, angry and arguing, and he saw the nervous one pacing back and forth in front of the fire.

"We told you just to watch her, dammit," he said. "Now she's going to be more on guard."

"I'm tired of watching her," the bald-headed one with the mustache growled.

"And now she's got herself a damn protector," the third one with the dyspeptic face put in. "All because you didn't follow orders."

"This bushwhacker that came in, you never saw him before?" the nervous man asked.

"Never."

The Trailsman stepped into the open, the big Sharps held in front of him. "His name's Fargo . . . Skye Fargo," he said, and the three men spun in surprise. He saw them start to move hands toward their guns. "I'm sure to get two of you," he said calmly. "Any volunteers?" The trio dropped the hands at their sides. "That's much smarter." Fargo smiled. "I just came to talk some. Drop your gun belts."

"I thought you said you came to talk," the tall one said.

"I talk better that way," Fargo said, and the trio reluctantly unbuckled their gun belts and let them slide to the ground. "You've got names. Let's have them."

"Why?" the tall one growled.

"I gave you my name," Fargo said cheerfully. "Besides, I ought to know your names if we're going to be partners."

"What the hell are you talking about?" the nervous one barked.

"*Names!*" Fargo snapped sharply.

"Ed Hauser," the nervous one said as his hands flicked across his shirt.

"Sam Brax," the tall, dyspeptic one said.

"Frank Dunn," the bald-headed, mustached man added.

"The little lady says she doesn't have what you boys are looking for," Fargo said.

"Bullshit," Sam Brax snapped back. "She knows where it is."

Fargo shrugged. "Maybe, maybe not. But I can find out," he said. The trio tossed him a stare of collective skepticism. "She trusts me now. I think I can get her to do more than just trust me. I can get her to level with me," he said. "But we have to have an understanding. I want a piece of the money if I find out where it is."

The trio exchanged glances.

"Maybe," the tall one said.

"And I want to know more. Why do you figure it's yours?" Fargo asked.

"We earned it. Fifteen years behind bars, that's why," Frank Dunn said.

"You stole it," Fargo said.

"We didn't exactly steal it. We caught onto this bank swindle back Kansas way, and we took the money and hid it. But they caught us and sent us up instead of the real swindlers. They wouldn't make a deal so we never told them where we hid the money," Hauser explained.

"How does the girl's pa figure into it?" Fargo asked.

"There were four of us. He was part of it," Sam Brax answered. "We decided he should be the one to hide the money."

"He served fifteen years with you?" Fargo asked.

"Fourteen, goddammit," Dunn snarled. "Charley Keller took sick and the doctors said he didn't have long to live. He was released a year before we got out.''

"And when you got out, you found he'd disappeared," Fargo said.

"That's right, the son of a bitch," Sam Brax roared.

Fargo frowned. A pandora's box of brand-new questions had suddenly been flung open, but he pushed them all aside for the moment. "None of this means the girl knows about the money. Maybe he went off and spent it," Fargo suggested.

"He didn't spend it. We checked that out when we looked for him. He didn't go anywhere, do anything, didn't buy any land or cattle or horses, didn't keep a fancy woman. He went and found his daughter and lived with her for the year we were still in prison," Dunn said.

"And told her where'd he'd hidden the money," Hauser added. "He expected that when he died we'd figure the money was gone. But we found out about the daughter. We know she knows where it is. That's why she ran off to live out here. He probably told her to lay low for a while."

Frank Dunn cut in, his voice full of frustrated anger. "But we tracked her down, goddammit, and she's going to tell us where that damn money is hidden," he roared.

"I get Charley Keller's share if I can get her to tell me where it is," Fargo said, and the three men exchanged glances.

It was Sam Brax who finally answered. "It's a deal," he said. "But don't get any smart ideas about grabbing it all for yourself."

"Wouldn't think of it," Fargo said. "I'll be in touch."

"Wait a minute, Fargo. How'd you come to be here?" Hauser asked.

"Broke trail for some church folks camped in the hollow. Got lucky, I guess." Fargo grinned.

"Don't take too long with the girl," Brax growled. "We're not waiting much longer."

"If she knows, I'll find out," Fargo said.

"She knows, goddammit," Dunn spit out.

Fargo shrugged as he lowered the rifle and walked away. He climbed onto the Ovaro as the three men scooped up their gun belts. He rode back across the low ridge and down into the hollow as he let his thoughts sort themselves out. He had convinced them he was an opportunist out to try to cut himself a slice of the pie, and he'd bought Diane Keller a little more time by it. Of course, they'd no intention of cutting him in for a share, but they'd nothing to lose by letting him try to find out about the money. They'd be keeping watch on Diane, anyway.

But as Fargo rode into the hollow, the other questions that had suddenly flown out of the darkness rose up again, and he thought about Leah's interest in the girl in the house. There were suddenly too many coincidences. It was time to press for answers, he figured as he dismounted in the trees away from the wagons. He undressed, pushing away a strangely ominous feeling that pulled at him, and slept.

When morning came, his eyes snapped open, a sense of danger gripping him. He moved slowly, half-turned on his side as his hand stole to the Colt beside him. His gaze swept the end of the hollow, then up along the rock and timber of the hill. He spied the four bronzed horsemen standing motionless midway up the hill. He followed their gaze and saw they were staring down at the campsite where Leah conducted the morning prayer service. The four Shoshoni remained as the service came to an end, and Fargo also watched the kneeling figures rise, the circle disband. His eyes went back to the Shoshoni. They remained in place, watching, then slowly, silently, they turned their ponies and vanished into the crevices of the hilly rock formations.

Fargo rose, his lips drawn back. They still watched and waited. He didn't understand why, but he was grateful for that much. Once again he'd been made aware that everything could be wiped away in an explosion of fury at any moment. He washed and dressed, walked to the campsite, and found Leah waiting for him with a mug of coffee. "I keep waiting to find you at prayer service," she said.

"It's hard for sinners to change habits," he said. "As hard as it is for good folks to tell them the whole truth."

Leah's eyes narrowed as she studied his bland expression. "What does that mean?" she asked finally.

"I visited the girl again. Her name's Diane Keller. It seems some folks think her pa hid twenty thousand dollars around here," Fargo said. "Sort of made me wonder."

He saw the caution come into her face. "Wonder what?" she asked.

"Whether that's why this is the chosen place," he slid out. "Seeing as how her pa was in jail for fourteen years, and Reverend Johnston preached in the jails."

She said nothing for a long moment, her face

carefully composed. "A sign was given the reverend," she said finally.

"Twenty thousand dollars is a lot of sign, I'll say that much," Fargo commented.

"You do not understand the workings of the spirit, Fargo," Leah said.

"I understand being conned," he snapped.

She seemed genuinely hurt by the accusation, the smoldering eyes growing wide with protest. "We did not do that," she said.

"Talking about a chosen place when you're really out after a bundle of cash is conning somebody," he growled.

"No, this is a chosen place. It will take time to explain it to you," she said.

"I've got time," he said.

"There is a pond at the edge of the hills. The women are waiting for me to go with them. Come back later, and we'll talk then," Leah said. "I can explain it to you then."

"Tonight," he grunted.

She nodded and searched his eyes. "I want you to understand. It is important to me," she said.

"I'll listen. But I wouldn't take bets on my understanding," he said, and walked away. He took the Ovaro rode only to the edge of the hills around the hollow. He traversed the entire perimeter of the hollow, his jaw set tight by the time he finished. There was no avenue out of the hollow that afforded any real protection. He turned the Ovaro up the low hill to the little house as the sun crossed into the afternoon sky and halted before it. He swung from the saddle and called out.

No one answered, but the door hung open and he stepped inside and called again. He received no answer. Two new drawings were spread out on the small table; one the delicate little blossoms of flowering spurge captured in simple lines; the other the vibrant scarlet of the cardinal flower set down in crayon. He stepped back outside just as she appeared from the other side of the hill, clad only in a towel that covered her torso and revealed lean, long legs and bare shoulders still glistening with drops of water.

"Didn't expect company at this hour," Diane said. "I've a private spring down there. She looked younger than she was, her lean legs giving her a coltish appearance, her bare shoulders without an ounce of extra flesh on them. She smiled at his appreciative gaze. "Thanks," she said. "I've never had a body that excites men."

"You'll do," he said.

"You talk while I dress," she said, stepping into the house, and he watched the towel move tightly across her lean little rear. He folded himself onto the doorstep as she called from inside the house. "Find out anything?" she asked.

"Enough. Maybe too much," he answered, and told her what the three men had revealed. She stepped out as he finished, a loose shirt on and a skirt she'd cut short, and he admired the long, lean firmness of her legs as she faced him. "So that's it. Your pa was in jail with them," Fargo concluded.

She half-shrugged. "It adds some pieces to the past, but it doesn't change anything else. I don't know where the money is hidden."

He pushed himself to his feet. "I think you do," he said, and saw the anger rush into her eyes at once.

"Go to hell. I thought you believed me," she snapped. "You can leave now."

"Simmer down," he said. "Didn't mean it the

way it sounded. I think you know without knowing you do." Her frown stayed, but the anger in her eyes faded a fraction. "It's plain he intended for you to have the money. He didn't tell you anything outright because he was waiting to see if Brax, Hauser, and Dunn would show up. If they did, he probably figured the less you knew, the better for you. But I'm sure he gave you hints, said things that meant something. I want you to think back about all the things he said during that year, maybe something that didn't make any sense to you at the time."

"I don't remember anything." Diane frowned.

"You won't, right off. You'll have to pull it out of yourself. But it's important you remember," Fargo said.

"I'll try."

"Try damn hard. We might run out of time any day. The Shoshoni are going to attack those wagons. When they do, it's likely your untouched existence up here will come to an end," Fargo said.

"You said they were church folks. Why are they staying here?" Diane asked.

Fargo's lips pursed. "They're after the money, too," he said, and saw Diane's mouth open in surprise. "I'll tell you more on that tomorrow, after I get some answers."

She stepped close to him and her arms came up to encircle his neck. "Thanks for helping, risking your neck, caring," she said. Her lips pressed his, a surprisingly gentle touch, and lingered for a sweet moment. "On account," she said.

"Good enough." He smiled. "Start thinking." He pressed her lean little rear, and she walked to the Ovaro with him as the day began to drift into dusk.

He swept the hills surrounding the hollow with a slow gaze, then swung onto the horse. She watched him ride down the hill, and he waved to her from halfway to the bottom. He put the pinto into a trot until he reached the campsite.

Darkness came quickly as supper was taken, and he saw Rachel meet his glance as she ate alone. Leah and Preacher Thomas conferred quietly during the meal. When Fargo finished, he took his bedroll deep into the trees and set his gear out. He slowly strolled back to the campsite where the wagons were already still and dark, but he saw a faint light from the converted milk wagon as he approached. The door slid open as he reached it, and he stepped inside where a candle in a tin cup gave a soft light that turned Leah's deep-blond hair into burnished gold.

She wore a light, pale-blue cottom robe, and the neckline let the swell of her breasts edge over the top. Fargo shook his head in frustration. The candlelight, the robe, her throbbing loveliness, it all went to waste, and he hated waste. "You're a damn fine-looking woman, Leah," he said. "You ought to pay more attention to that."

"When it is time," she answered.

"Hell, you don't give time a chance," he muttered.

"I want to explain everything to you, Fargo," she said firmly. "I don't want you to feel that we have untruthful to you."

"I don't think you've got time to do that, but you can try," he commented coldly.

"A sign is a message. A sign must be recognized. Sometimes it comes as it did to Saul on the road to Damascus, but most of the time it is given through the ways of men and worldly things. It was meant for us to come here. That is why this is a chosen place, just as the money is ours."

"Yours?" He frowned.

"To do the work of the Church. The sign was given us," Leah said. "Everyone here knows it. Everyone here is anxious to spread the word of the Church."

"How can you be so damn sure you got a sign?" Fargo questioned.

"Because otherwise what happened would not have happened," Leah answered.

He blinked, started to probe the logic of the answer, and quickly stopped. They followed a reasoning that excluded logic and replaced it with something that was either inner conviction or convenience. "Just exactly what was this sign?" he asked.

"When Reverend Johnston preached to Charles Keller in prison, Keller was a very sick man. He thought he was about to die then. He told Reverend Johnston about the money he had hidden away, and he described this place. He was sick with the fever and almost delirious, but he was very clear in his description. However, the fever passed and Charles Keller improved. When Reverend Johnston questioned him about what he'd told him when he thought he was dying, Keller denied it. He said it had all been due to the fever."

"But Reverend Johnston figured he had told the truth," Fargo put in, and Leah nodded.

"There was no doubt about that," she said. "Reverend Johnston had to go on to another prison, but he planned to return and talk to Charles Keller again."

"But while the reverend was preaching in the

other prisons Charley Keller was released a year early and disappeared," Fargo finished.

"Exactly," Leah said. "Reverend Johnston tried to track him down and discovered that he'd lived with his daughter and that the daughter had left to go somewhere alone after he died. We knew it had to be here."

Fargo grunted silently. The story fitted in with that of the three other searchers for the money. "So you went searching for this place," he muttered.

"The sign had been given us," Leah said.

"Charley Keller ranting with fever was the sign," Fargo said.

"Yes. I told you, signs come mostly through the works of men. We had been told about the money because it was meant to be ours, to further the work of the Church," Leah said.

"You really believe that, don't you?" Fargo frowned.

"There is no question about it," Leah said.

"It's likely you're going to be massacred by the Shoshoni," he said. "Will that be a sign, too?"

"They will not massacre us. They have not attacked yet, and they will not," Leah said.

She carried such conviction that it almost made him willing to toss aside reason and the things he knew about the Shoshoni. He could see how a powerful preaching man such as Rev. Johnston could carry others along with his fervor and conviction. "What if there is no money?" he asked.

"There is. The girl knows where it is," Leah said.

"She says she doesn't," he answered.

"She does," Leah said. "We would not have been sent here otherwise."

Fargo grunted. Everybody was sure Diane knew

where the money was hidden. Brax and the others thirsted for it out of pure greed, Leah and the disciples out of the certainty they had been given a divine right to it. It didn't much matter. Neither was about to give up. He looked at Leah, found her smoldering eyes studying him.

"I've tried to make you understand," she said.

"Understanding's not the same as agreeing," he told her. He rose, and she stood up with him. As he bent his head forward to avoid hitting the roof of the milk wagon, he smelled the faintly musky woman smell of her and a hint of soap tinted with rose petal. He lowered his head, pressed his lips on hers, and though she didn't respond, she didn't pull away either. He kissed her gently, pressed harder, and finally pulled back. The smoldering eyes stared up at him. "Maybe your body's a sign. Ever think of that?" he asked.

"I have thought about things you've said," Leah answered, and her hands came up to rest against his chest. "I want you to help us find the money. But you are still unconvinced you should be one of us. I must change that." He saw her lips part as she reached up and pressed her mouth on his. She held him, letting herself enjoy the before pulling back.

"How about just enjoying yourself," he said.

She shrugged. "If that is to be part of it," she said.

"Oh, it sure is, honey," he said. "But it's a little cramped in here. Come with me. I've got my bedroll all laid out by the far cedars."

"Go and wait for me. I will come," she said.

"All right." He pulled the door open and hopped down from the wagon. He hurried through the night to where he'd left his bedroll in the cedars, still wrestling with surprise. She had come around with unexpected suddenness. She'd given herself a reason, of course, the need to convince him. If she wanted to see screwing as one more sign, that was fine with him. He started to pull off his shirt when he heard a whispered call. He halted and peered through the trees. "Over here," he said, and strained his eyes to see the figure appear and hurry toward him in a gray nightshirt.

"Surprise," she said.

"Rachel." He swallowed. "Christ, get out of here."

Her face fell into an instant pout. "I decided the hell with all of them," she said.

"Leah's due here any minute, dammit," he said, and it was Rachel's turn for openmouthed surprise. "She's coming to talk to me about the girl on the hill and convince me to help her find the money," he said.

Rachel straightened, disappointment tightening her mouth. "Damn," she said. "I could come back?"

"Not tonight," he hissed.

"At least you won't be enjoying yourself any more than I will," she said as she turned and started through the trees.

"Go around the long way," he called, and saw her shift direction before she faded from sight. He let a deep rush of air escape his lips as he sat down on the bedroll and pulled off his shirt. He'd just taken off boots when he heard a rustle of foliage. He rose, called out, and in the dim moonlight caught a gleam of the deep-blond hair. Leah came through the trees, her eyes instantly taking in the muscled beauty of his chest.

She wore the robe pulled tight around herself,

and she halted in front of him. She lowered her arms and opened the robe, letting it fall to the ground to stand completely naked before him. He stared, taken aback at the absolute beauty of her. Her body was more gorgeous than he'd expected. Full, round breasts, curved magnificently with full red nipples surrounded by large deep-pink circles. Her ribs were rounded and curved down into a narrow waist, and her belly slightly convex. Underneath was her dense triangle of black wiry curls and full-thighed legs that flexed sinuously into lovely calves. Everything about her was ripe and fairly pulsating with full bloom. Damn, he murmured inwardly, his own virgin goddess.

"I wait for you, Fargo," Leah said, her eyes half-closed.

"Not for long," he muttered as he felt his maleness already trying to fight out of his trousers. He shed clothes, took her shoulders in his hands, and brought her down to the bedroll. Her arms encircled him, and her mouth was open and waiting as he pressed his lips to her. He let his tongue dart forward, surrogate penetration as he curled his hand around one full, beautiful breast. He rubbed his thumb over the red little tip and felt it rise, grow firm, almost quiver. He bent low, caressed her breasts with his lips, drew one into his mouth, and circled the red tip with his tongue.

"Oooooh," Leah murmured, the sound so low he could hardly hear it. He pulled and sucked and caressed, and Leah's voice rose in strength. He felt her body begin to move slowly, sinuously. Her legs lifted, came down again, lifted again, rubbing together as her hips moved in a rotating motion. "Lord, oh, Lord," she said breathlessly.

He let his hands explore the warmth of her body,

move down the throbbing sinuousness of her as she continued to move. Her lips opened, her eyes remained closed as he touched, pressed, and caressed, and her low moaning sounds grew deeper, fuller. He brought his body over hers, pressed his rigid fullness into her curly triangle, and her legs rose, fell open, and she gave a gasped moan. Her hands tightened against his shoulders. "Come to me," Leah said. "Come to me, Fargo." He heard the note of urgent demand in her moan.

But he held back, sucked on her breasts again, and his hand reached down to touch her moist warmth. "Oh, Fargo. It is right. Lord, yes, yes," Leah gasped out, and he drew his hand away and felt her shudder, tighten against him at once. "No, no, stay . . . stay," she said breathlessly, but this time he brought his turgid organ to her and slid into her moist warmth. "Oh, Lord," Leah murmured, and though he found no tightness to her, he moved slowly, carefully.

"All right?" he asked, and she clasped her hands hard against him.

"Yes. Do not be afraid," Leah said. "The body follows the spirit. The way is made smooth."

He pressed deeper and frowned. Maybe there was more to it than he realized, for he found only smooth, warm, and enveloping pleasure. He plunged harder, drew back, plunged again, and Leah moaned. Her sinuous writhing grew stronger, matched his every thrust. Her hands dug into him and her full thighs were soft against his sides. "It is good, it is right," Leah murmured, her voice low, her moans deep. She moved beneath him and her throbbingly beautiful body rubbed against him, the magnificent breasts falling from side to side as she half-turned, pressed, turned again.

"Fargo," she said with sudden sharpness. "Fargo!" Her voice rose, his name called out with sudden demand and a hint of panic. He felt her sinuous writhing halt and her body begin to quiver, throb against him. He pumped quickly, his own body sensing the onrush of the senses, and Leah clutched him.

"Fargo," she cried out again. "Oh, Lord. Aaaaaaaah," she cried, and rose up, her back arching, her moaning cry hanging in the air. He pushed his pelvis hard against her dense, curly pubic hair, and he heard the moan of fulfillment curl inside her half-scream as she came with him. He held her at the peak of her ecstasy, pumped hard, and kept her there as long as he could, until finally she let herself fall back onto the bedroll. He lay atop her and looked at her face: her eyes closed, her lips parted, her cheeks flushed. He saw ecstasy, pleasure, and satisfaction in her lovely countenance, along with a kind of fulfilled peace. But no smile. Dammit, he swore silently. No smile.

Leah opened her eyes to look at him and saw the frown on his face. She lifted her hand to smooth it from his brow. "It was a wonderful thing because it was right," she said.

"If you say so," Fargo answered, and rested on one elbow as she sat up. He enjoyed the full, womanly, sensual beauty of her. She stretched and the deep, full breasts lifted in gorgeous magnificence. "Tell me something. Why was it right for you and not for Rachel?" he asked.

Her blue eyes looked at him with almost chiding disbelief. "Because Rachel came to you only for the flesh, for the carnal pleasures," Leah said. "I came here because I realized it was the only way to reach you. My body preached to you, Fargo."

Fargo let his lips purse. "Best damn sermon I ever had," he said.

Leah smiled.

6

Leah reached for the robe, and Fargo pulled it away and saw the protest in her eyes. "Immodesty is a sin," she said. "It's wrong to display oneself."

"Bullshit," Fargo snapped. "Beauty is a gift, not a sin. Is it wrong for a rose to display itself, a scarlet tanager to show its gorgeous colors, a beautiful filly to stand proud?"

"You have a way of seeing things differently, I'll admit," she said, and rested on one elbow. The full breasts dipped down with provocatively beautiful lines. "I do not feel modesty with you," she said.

"Good." He grinned.

"I want you to go to the girl, again, Fargo," Leah said as her breasts brushed his chest. "Convince her to tell you where the money is hidden. She must tell you."

"Must?" Fargo echoed.

"None of us has any choice in the matter. It is foreordained. The sign was given and called us here," Leah said.

Fargo let his hand move across the smooth skin of her broad back. He pressed her forward and cupped one full breast with his other hand. "You going to preach to me again?" he whispered, and heard Leah's sharp intake of breath as he caressed the deep-red tip.

"I don't know if it will be right," she murmured.

"It'll be right. One sermon wouldn't do a sinner such as me," Fargo said, and pulled her to him, pressing his face into the full breasts. He heard Leah's little moan as her arms encircled him and held his face against her. His mouth found the red tip of one breast and drew it in, and Leah came with him as he rolled onto his back, still sucking the round, soft mound.

"How good," Leah murmured. "The body serves. Ah, yes, yes." She half-rose and rolled, pulling him with her, and he felt her hands moving frantically up and down his sides. He reached down, caught her wrist, brought his already pulsating organ up, and placed it into her hand. She half-screamed, started to draw away, but he held her there. Her half-scream became a soft cry, and he felt her fingers tighten around him. "Oh, my," Leah whispered.

"Staff of pleasure, honey," Fargo murmured.

"Yes, yes," she gasped. "Oh, yes." He took his hand from her wrist, and she continued to hold him, moving her fingers along his throbbing warmth. She slowly pulled on him, brought him down to the dense, curly triangle, and opened the firm, full-fleshed thighs. "Come to me, Fargo, come to me," she murmured, and he moved into her wanting, hot passage. He slid forward gently and felt her back arch. "More, more." Leah sighed, and he moved deeper, harder, faster, until suddenly the night exploded again, and he heard her low, groaning moans of pleasure.

She lay beside him later, and the warm glow of her subsided slowly as she sat up. He watched the flush in her face fade away, the sensual lips pull in firmly as she put the robe on. Her eyes met his, and he saw something close to triumphant satisfaction in their smoldering depths.

"You'll see to the girl tomorrow, won't you, Fargo?" Leah said as he got to his feet with her.

"I'll try," he said. "Can't promise anything."

"You'll find out for us. You know now that it must be," Leah said, and pulled the robe more tightly around her. "Good night, Fargo," she said, and he watched her walk away, a firm, almost regal air to her. She disappeared into the trees, and he lay down with a frown wrinkling his brow. Leah had given fully and she had enjoyed, her beautiful body thoroughly caught up in the newly awakened pleasures of the flesh. Yet he had the feeling he hadn't made her see with new eyes, feel with new senses, come to a new awareness of herself. It was as if she really believed she had preached with her loins instead of her lips. He went to sleep feeling strangely uncomfortable, not unlike a man who has had a marvelous meal that somehow failed to satisfy.

When morning came, the sense of danger seized him again, and this time he immediately gazed up at the hillside. He saw again the four Shoshoni on their ponies, but they had moved considerably lower down the hillside, their eyes fastened on the circle where Leah held the morning prayer service. He saw one gesture as the Indians continued to peer intently at the campsite as the service came to an end. The disciples rose and began to drift to a small breakfast fire, and Fargo watched as the Shoshoni waited a few moments longer, then faded into the trees and passages of the hill.

He turned away, his own frown digging into his brow. Their actions still didn't make any sense. He washed, dressed, gathered his things, and walked to the campsite. Mary Carlton gave him a mug of coffee, and he saw Rachel's eyes on him as she leaned against a wagon wheel. Leah stepped forward as he entered the camp and put his things on the Ovaro. He watched her scan the others, the usual firmness in her face but a quiet hint of triumph in her eyes.

"I have news," she said. "Brother Fargo is going to get the girl to tell us where the money is hidden," she said, and Fargo frowned at the murmur of approval that went through the half-circle of listeners. "Brother Fargo knows time is important," Leah said. "I've told him how you are impatient to go forward with the work of the Church. He will press her for answers."

"Amen," someone said.

"Amen," Ruth Classoon echoed, and Fargo went to Leah as the others began to drift away.

"You didn't tell me you were going to make announcements," he said with irritation.

"The faithful must know everything," she said.

"I didn't make any promises, dammit. I told you she says she doesn't know anything about the money."

"And we know she is lying," Leah said firmly. Fargo put aside the subject, his eyes searching Leah's face. She met his gaze with clear-eyed firmness.

"Things any different this morning?" he slid at her.

"Every morning is different," she said. "Find out about the girl." She turned and strode away. He frowned as he started for the Ovaro. He had reached the horse when he saw Rachel coming toward him, her eyes narrowed as she peered at him.

"Brother Fargo?" she commented, hands on hips.

He shrugged. "You know Leah's way with words," he said.

But suspicion didn't leave the hazel eyes. "What the hell happened last night?" Rachel questioned sharply.

Fargo did not reply.

Rachel's eyes continued to bore into him. "Brother Fargo," she repeated. "Brother Fargo's going to help us. She came on to you last night, didn't she?" Fargo tightened the cinch ring on the saddle and cursed the unfailing power of the female intuition. "I'll be damned," Rachel muttered. "Miss Pure and Mighty gave out. I'll be damned."

"Now, don't go running off at the bit," Fargo said, but Rachel was staring at Leah's wagon. She pulled her eyes back to him, and he saw her round face grow tight.

"I'll tell you one thing: if you think a roll in the hay changed her, you're all wrong," Rachel snapped. She whirled and strode away.

Fargo swung onto the pinto and rode from camp with the gut feeling that there was more truth than anger in Rachel's words. He rode to the little hill, climbed the gentle slope, and spotted Diane halfway down the west slope, sitting on the grass with her sketch pad in hand. He rode up and saw she was putting the deep-pink vibrancy of a steeplebush on paper. She halted as he came up, her smile quick and warm. She had on a pale-blue shirt that rested lightly on the smallish breasts, two faint points pressing themselves forward.

"Come up with anything?" he asked sourly as he dismounted.

"Not a thing," Diane said. "Is that all you came up for?"

"Yes, dammit," he barked. "I suggest you stop drawing and start thinking."

"You mean, just sit around all day thinking?" Diane frowned.

"If you have to," he returned. "You're running out of time, honey." She folded the sketch pad and frowned at him. "I found out more," Fargo said. "He told Reverend Johnston about the money when he thought he was going to die in prison. Now, the reverend's disciples see that as a sign from above. They feel they were given the divine right to the money. It's theirs, awarded them by God."

"I don't believe this," Diane murmured.

"You'd best damn well believe it," Fargo said. "It means you've got three desperate sidewinders on one hand and a bunch of religious crazies on the other, all of whom are sure you know where the money is hidden and none about to wait much longer to come after you for it."

Diane came to him, put one hand on his chest. "Thanks for wanting to help. But I haven't been able to remember anything that might even fit," she said.

"Stop trying to remember something that fits," he told her. "Lay down in the house alone, let your mind go backward. Think about the year you spent together. Think about the little things. Don't strain at it."

She reached up, brushed his cheek with a light kiss. "I'll try," she said. "You going to stay awhile?"

"No, I'm going to scout some. Maybe I can find a

way that'll let us sneak out of here, and to hell with all of them," he said. "I'll stop back later."

"All right," she said, and he waited till she went into the little house before he rode down the south side of the hill. He slowly headed up the low ridge at the south end of the hollow and spied Sam Brax's tall, rangy figure sitting astride the horse at the edge of a line of blue spruce. He steered the pinto toward the man and reached the top of the ridge. He reined to a halt to meet the man's sour stare.

"I don't like being watched," Fargo said. "I told you I'd talk to her in my time and my way."

"Been waiting, not watching," Sam Brax said. "We were talking last night and got us some questions. Those missionary folks you brought here, they're after the money, too, aren't they?"

Fargo kept his face bland. "Now, what makes you think that?" he asked.

"The boys and me remembered about a preacher that kept going to visit Charley in jail when he first took real sick," Sam Brax said.

"The Reverend Johnston." Fargo nodded. "It seems one day Charley Keller felt he needed to confess his sins, and he told the reverend about the money."

"The damn fool," Sam Brax spit out. "That settles it. We're not waiting around any longer."

"Give me a chance. You've waited this long," Fargo said placatingly. Another voice cut in from halfway in back of him.

"Drop your gun, Fargo," it said, and he turned to see Ed Hauser holding rifle aimed at him. The crack of a twig on the other side made him turn half around to see Frank Dunn's bald pate shining in the sun, a big .52-caliber Spencer in his hands.

"You're making a mistake. Give me another day with her, and I'll have the answer for you," Fargo said.

"Or for your missionary friends," Sam Brax muttered.

"I told you I'm not part of them," Fargo said.

"We're not taking any chances. Drop the goddamn gun," Brax snarled, and Fargo carefully lifted the Colt from its holster and let it fall to the ground. "Get off the horse. This side," Hauser ordered, and Fargo swung down to the ground. He had just touched the grass when he felt a rush of air. He tried to turn away, but the stock of the heavy Spencer crashed into the back of his head. He fell forward as the Ovaro skittered aside. He tried to get up, but another blow smashed into his skull. The world exploded in a pinwheel of orange flashes, then a smothering blanket of grayness swept over him. He shook his head and felt another blow, and the grayness became an inky void. He lay on his face, and dim sounds penetrated the inky blackness, voices that seemed very far away.

"Throw him over the edge," one of the voices said.

"Let's get the goddamn bitch and make her talk."

The voices vanished, and he lay still in the void. He didn't feel himself lifted and carried. He didn't feel his body roll down the steep side of the ridge, crashing hard into trees and rocks in its headlong descent. There was only the void—soundless, timeless, formless, a place that might have been death. He knew nothing, felt nothing. There was only the empty void, total nothingness.

It seemed sudden when it came, the wetness.

Only it wasn't sudden at all, the senses holding out meaning. The wetness stayed, seeped into his awareness, and then the pain came, stabbing bursts of it throughout his body. He had never realized that pain could be a happy thing, but he felt the spiral of joy gather inside himself. He could feel, and only the living could feel. He forced his eyes open and the world was blurred, shapeless. He blinked, closed his eyes, forced them open again, and the gray blurred shapes began to take form. The wetness stayed, but it flowed only over half his face, he realized.

Slowly he raised his head and let objects grow clear. He lay in water, too deep to be a stream, not large enough to be a river. His head had rested on a flat rock just below the surface of the water, he saw. It had kept half his face out of the water. Six inches and he would have drowned, his head entirely under the flowing water. He pushed himself up with the palms of his hands, his body crying out in protest. He sat up, drew a deep breath as the water flower around his legs. He sat in a crystalline fissure, he realized. The water flowed through it from a waterfall somewhere higher in one of the hills. He lifted his eyes; the sun had started down beyond the horizon. He had lain unconscious all damn day, he swore with sudden realization. His gaze traveled up the steep side of rock and trees from where he'd been thrown, and he understood why his body throbbed with pain.

He tried to clear his head and remember. He heard the dim voices again. They had gone to get Diane. He cursed as he pulled himself to his feet. He stumbled along the bottom of the steep sides of rock, half in the water and half out, until he found a place that seemed to offer a chance to climb up.

He began to pull himself along by the tough, scraggly brush that protruded. Wedging fingers and feet into cracks and crevices, he fought down the pain of his body as he climbed.

He had to rest often, and he was breathing hard when he finally reached the top of the ridge. He crawled onto the ridge just as night swept over the land. He lay prone until his breath returned, and then pushed himself to his feet. He worked his way back to where the trio had bushwhacked him. He dropped to one knee whistled, and waited. The Ovaro materialized almost immediately, trotting up from the far side of the ridge. He pulled himself painfully into the saddle and set the pinto down into the hollow.

They had taken the big Sharps from its saddle holster, he saw. When he reached the small hill inside the hollow, he let the Ovaro race up the slope, and the little house was dark as he approached it.

He dropped to the ground outside the open door and let the first rays of the moonlight the hoofprints that led down the back side of the hill. They'd taken her from the house, and he began to follow the hoofprints. He walked, at first, then swung onto the Ovaro when the moon rose higher, following the tracks into the thicker woodland at the edge of the hollow. He walked the Ovaro slowly, paused to listen with almost every step.

The murmur of voices came to him first, punctuated by a sharp cry of pain from Diane. He followed the sound, leaving the Ovaro tethered to a low branch, and moved closer on foot. He crouched, wincing at the pain in his ribs. He saw movement through the trees to his right and the glow of a very small fire. He crept forward. Diane was tied to a tree with her arms pulled back to half-encircle the trunk. Her face in the glow of the small fire bore red bruise marks. Frank Dunn faced her, his bald head glistening. "Goddamn you, lady, we'll beat the hell out of you unless you talk," he heard the man snarl.

"Don't know anything," Diane murmured, pain in her voice.

Fargo crept closer and saw that the pale-blue blouse hung open in front, and he saw more red bruise marks at the base of her neck. They had plainly been working on her to get their answer and, of course, had gotten no place. His lips drew back in a grimace as he saw Dunn turn to the other two.

"That's enough. Let's work her over good," the man rasped.

"Not so much she can't answer us," Ed Hauser cautioned.

"She'll answer," Dunn said, and walked over to his horse. Fargo saw him return with a short-handled whip, which he waved in front of Diane's face. "You want to talk, or do I scar every goddamn inch of you?" he roared.

Diane shook her head again and Fargo saw the pleading in her eyes. "I don't know anything," she said. "I don't, I don't."

The man loosed a stream of curses at her as Fargo's eyes swept the small cleared spot, scaning the edges for anything he could use as a weapon. He grimaced again as he saw nothing. He knelt on one knee and drew the thin, double-edged throwing knife from the calf holster around his leg. He could take out one with it, but that left the other two time to draw and blaze away at him. Even if he threw the knife from the cover of the trees, they'd know he was there. His one advantage of surprise would be shattered. He had to take out more than one with his first move, and he shifted his position as Frank Dunn stepped back from Diane, raised the whip in his hand. Hauser and Sam Brax were standing very close together, Hauser almost behind the taller, sour-faced Brax. Both of them were only a few feet from the fire. Fargo moved through the trees as silent as a cougar on the prowl, even though he ached with every step.

He stopped when he reached a spot almost directly behind Hauser, and he saw Dunn send the whip lashing through the air. Diane screamed as it tore across her waist. Fargo cursed silently as he forced his eyes to stay on the two men near the fire. He measured distances, crept another six inches closer. Dunn was raising the whip again when Fargo pulled his arm back. He started to hurtle forward as he sent the razor-sharp, double-edged blade whistling through the air. He had time only to glimpse it plunge into the back of Dunn's neck as he crashed into the open, hit Ed Hauser from behind with the full force of his hurtling form. His shoulders slammed into the small of Hauser's back and the man catapulted into the tall, rangy figure in front of him. Sam Brax fell face forward into the fire and his scream of pain drowned out the soft, gurgling noises that came from the figure that lay on the ground with the knife handle sticking up from his neck.

Hauser fell half sideways, avoiding the fire. He landed on his side and rolled and Fargo dived for the man as he saw Hauser yank his gun out. He missed but got a glancing blow in against Hauser's cheek, and the man's shot whistled past his shoulder. Instead of rolling away, Fargo flung himself into Hauser as the man tried to bring the gun around. His shot went wild again, and Fargo jammed his forearm into the man's throat and Hauser went backward, his eyes bulging. A long, looping right crashed into the middle of his face, and Fargo felt the bone in his nose crack. As Hauser went limp, Fargo heard the shots explode and bullets kick up soil too close. He saw Sam Brax, part of his face hanging red and raw with little pieces of charred skin dangling. The man fired bullets with more pain and rage than accuracy, but a stray bullet could kill as effectively as a well-aimed one, Fargo reminded himself as he rolled again to avoid the hail of lead.

He came up against a tree, leapt to his feet as Sam Brax staggered, tried to reload, dropped the bullets as he stuffed them into the revolver's chambers, all the while moaning in pain. Fargo rushed the tall figure, charging in a low crouch, but he saw the man raise the gun and he dived flat as two bullets passed over him. He hit Sam Brax at the ankles, and the man fell forward over him. Fargo whirled on the ground as he heard the scream of anguish. Sam Brax had fallen facedown on a piece of burning firewood that had been knocked away from the fire. The man screamed again as he rolled onto his back, and the screams trailed off into a succession of quivering moans.

Sam Brax's face was no longer dyspeptic. It just wasn't there. He gave a final quiver as Fargo pushed himself to his feet and crossed to where Diane stared, pain still in her eyes. He untied her bonds and she fell against him to cling for a long moment, and when she stepped back, her eyes held less pain.

"They told me they'd killed you," she said.

"They almost did," Fargo said, not without bitterness. "My fault. I let them surprise me."

Diane cast a glance around the little glen and shuddered. "Let's get out of here," she said, and he nodded.

He went to retrieve the slender throwing knife, his big Colt, which was stuck into Brax's belt, and the rifle that had been put onto Dunn's horse. Hauser was the only one still alive. He'd wake up to a broken nose and a badly bruised larynx, but he'd be alive, and grateful for that. It was unlikely he'd do anything more than hightail it. Fargo put the rifle back in its saddle holster and followed Diane onto the horse. She saw him wince in pain.

"They tossed me down a cliffside," he explained as her eyes questioned.

"I've some ointment that'll work wonders. Comfrey, hyssop, and balm of gilead," she said.

He started to send the Ovaro back through the woods when he caught the faint sound and reined up. He sat silently, his ears straining, and his jaw grew tight. He pulled the horse around and moved toward the hillside.

"What is it?" Diane frowned.

"Listen," he murmured as he sent the Ovaro up along a trail that climbed the hill, snaked behind rocks, and curved beside a line of blue spruce. They'd gone halfway up the big hill before she caught what his wild-creature hearing had heard.

"Drums," Diane murmured, and turned to toss him an apprehensive frown.

He slid from the saddle with her, left the Ovaro, and started to climb forward on foot. The sound of the drums grew louder as he climbed, Diane staying close to him. They hadn't gone very far when the land began to flatten. A small mountain plateau formed with its own set of rocks, crags, and mountain brush. A bonfire blazed at the far end of it, and Fargo focused on the near-naked figures that formed a circle around the flames while two others beat hide drums in the background. Fargo lay flat behind a line of brush, Diane pressed against his side as he watched the Shoshoni pass among them an object with beaver tail and otter skin dangling from each end.

"What are they doing?" Diane whispered.

"Passing the medicine bundle," Fargo said. "So everyone can take strength and protection from it in battle."

"Does that mean they're ready to attack?" Diane asked.

"Can't say for sure. Sometimes these ceremonial preparations go on for days," he told her. "They keep holding back for some reason I haven't figured out yet."

Just then, one of the figures around the fire rose, extended his arms skyward, and stepped out of the circle to begin a slow, deliberate dance around the others. He made a complete circle around the perimeter of those seated by the fire.

"The medicine man," Fargo murmured. "He'd be the first to dance." As the medicine man resumed his place around the fire, another of the braves rose and began to dance in slow, foot-stomping steps. "Let's go. I've seen enough," Fargo said, and he began to slide backward down the hillside. Diane slid down beside him until they reached the place where he'd left the Ovaro. They climbed on, and he sent the horse down the creviced hillside. When they reached bottom, he turned the horse through the timber and finally out onto the hollow, where he took the Ovaro up the gentle hill to the little house.

Diane swung to the ground first and hurried into the house ahead of him. "I'll start a fire," she said. By the time he had finished unsaddling the Ovaro, the house was warmed by a fire.

"Why'd they take you away from the house?" he asked as he entered.

"They were afraid some of your missionary group might decide to come up after me," Diane answered, and he saw her face grow grave. "I think maybe I'm afraid of that, too, now. I guess I've become afraid of everyone."

"They'll hold off some. I'm supposed to be getting you to tell me where the money is hidden," Fargo said. "I'll have to report back, come morning, and play them along a little more."

"That's come morning. Right now you need a rubdown for those aches and bruises. Take off those wet clothes and lay down on the bed," Diane said, and gestured to a mattress on a pallet in the far corner of the room.

He hurt more than enough not to protest, and as Diane rummaged in a corner, he undressed almost to complete nakedness and lay down on the mattress on his stomach. Diane came over to him with a small, earthen jar, poured a little of its contents into the palms of her hands, and began to rub it over his shoulders and back. He groaned happily at the warm, soothing touch of both hands and ointment. Diane's hands smoothed his skin and dug gently into his muscles. She gave a damn fine rubdown, he decided as she rubbed, stroked, and massaged his knotted muscles.

"How'd you get so good?" he asked.

"An artist studies anatomy," she answered, and

he nodded as he felt his eyelids growing heavy under the soothing magic of her touch and the penetrating warmth of the ointment. He tried to stay awake but instead felt himself drifting into the welcome embrace of sleep. He gave up the struggle, and the sleep of exhaustion held him in its grip. He slept soundly, aware only of the peace of warm and restful slumber.

He woke before dawn and stretched, his eyes still closed, and his body responded with only a twinge of pain. The room was warm and still, and it seemed as though Diane's hands were still rubbing, stroking, massaging, only now they were moving along the inside of his thighs, up onto his dormant maleness. The fantasy seemed so real that he let himself enjoy the remainder of it as he could almost feel her gentle yet firm touch. He realized he was responding, rising to the excitement that stirred inside him, and suddenly he felt the smooth touch of skin against his leg. He opened his eyes and pushed up on one elbow to see Diane's naked form half over his groin, her hand holding his growing organ, stroking, smoothing.

She felt him move, looked up, and her smile was slightly sly. "Sorry, couldn't resist it," she murmured.

"I say anything about objecting?" he replied.

She smiled again and continued to hold him in her hand. He let himself take in her lean figure, not an ounce of excess flesh on her anywhere, ribs showing, shoulders a trifle bony, but the smallish breasts stood up saucily, concavely curved at the tops but turning up nicely at the bottoms. Pink-brown nipples on pink areolae thrust forward and a tight stomach led down to an almost flat little pubic mound with a wire-mat triangle. Her legs were lean, yet surprisingly sexy in a young-colt way. All of her radiated its own kind of provocativeness, a wiry, spare beauty not unlike the beauty of a tight-bodied, lean filly.

He reached down and drew her up to him. He found her lips open and waiting, and her tongue darted out instantly with a wildness that surprised him. He responded, let the moist, warm surrogate penetrations excite them both. She lifted her face from his, scooted up, and thrust one breast into his mouth. Diane Keller cried out as she rotated her breast inside his mouth, leaning deeper into him, then pulling back. Her lean legs came up to clamp around him and rubbed hard against his now-seeking, waving organ. His hands could easily circle the narrow, thin rib cage, and he held her tight as she wriggled against him. Her hands moved down to his throbbing organ, clasped it, and she half-wriggled from his grasp and positioned herself under him as she kept her grip. He felt her lean legs come open, moved with her as she drew him to her.

"Let me. Oh, let me," she said breathlessly as she guided him into her, pulling his pulsating shaft inside her. He heard her little cry of pleasure.

Diane's hands fell to her side as he moved forward inside her, and she cried out in delight. "So good," she murmured as he moved harder inside her, drew back, slid forward, matching his movements to her quick gasps of joy. Diane's lean legs curled around his waist, and she tightened leg muscles to pull him in deeper with his every thrust. She used her arms to pull herself up and against him as if she could will her flesh and his to join together, exchange skins, senses, hungers. Fargo moved faster with her as her lean body became a writhing, pushing, twisting instrument of pleasure. Little gasped sounds came from her mouth, which pressed into his shoulder. Suddenly he heard the gasped sounds take on a new pitch, a higher, more urgent sound, and her body clung with new fervor to him.

"Now, now," Diane called, and her back drew up into an arch. He saw her head fall back, her eyes staring with the wildness of frenetic fervor as the moment swept onto her, consuming, carrying the world away. "Aaaah," Diane half-groaned as the moment began to spiral downward, and she sank back to hold him to her almost as a consolation.

As he sank down across her lean body, she turned, lifted, and put one of her breasts into his mouth and stayed there against him until she finally rolled onto her back. Then she curled up next to him on the mattress as the first light of day slid into the little house. He lay with her for a while, then rose to wash and dress.

Diane stayed curled up on the mattress until he had dressed. She stretched, and he had to fight down the urge to return to her. She reached out and found a shirt and slipped it on, swung the long, lean legs gracefully over the edge of the mattress, and stood up. "What are you going to tell them?" she asked as she came to him.

"That I'm getting real close to you." He grinned.

She laughed. "That's no lie," she agreed, and her face suddenly grew serious. "What if they decide not to wait any longer, the way Hauser and the others did?"

"It's the Shoshoni not waiting that worries me," Fargo said as Diane walked to the door with him. "If they hit the warpath, they'll include you in, I'm thinking. Is there anyplace you can hide?"

"There are two tall, narrow caves at the base of the west hill, hidden by a half-dozen big spruce. I explored them once. I could hide out there," Diane answered.

"You may have to," Fargo said, grimness in his voice. "I'll get back as soon as I can."

Diane kissed him quickly in the doorway.

He hurried to the Ovaro and saddled the horse as the new day flooded the hollow. He rode across the small flat top of the hill, started down the other side, and reined to a halt. He could see the campsite below, Leah conducting the morning prayer service, everyone gathered around her, kneeling in a circle. He also saw the four Shoshoni. They had come down still closer to the bottom of the hillside, and as he watched, he saw two of them lift their arms, fists closed, and gesture with obvious contempt at the wagons. When they turned away this time, they made no effort to silently fade into the hillside but spurred their ponies upward with sharp whoops and cries.

Fargo stared down at the prayer service circle as the frown formed in his brow. "Shit," he muttered. It had been there all the time and he hadn't put it together till now. He cursed again as he wheeled the horse around, raced back up the hill to the little house. Diane saw him returning and came out, buttoning on her skirt.

"Get whatever you want to take with you," he said. "Watch the hillsides. When you see the Shoshoni start to come down, you sneak out of here to those caves. Think you can do it?"

"I'll do it," she said. "Stay. Come with me."

He looked back down into the hollow. "I've got to warn them," he said. "But you go when you get the chance. I'll find you. Stay in those caves no matter what."

Her eyes were grave. "What if you don't come?"

"Wait the night through," he told her, and there was no need to spell out more. He sent the pinto into a gallop as he turned and raced down the low hill into the campsite just as the prayer service ended.

Leah came toward him as he swung from the horse, and the others gathered behind her. Rachel, to one side, watched with almost amused interest.

"You've learned where she has hidden the money?" Leah asked.

"I learned the Shoshoni are going to attack. Get into your wagons and get the hell out of this hollow fast," Fargo said.

"They are not going to attack. We have seen them watching. They are only observing. You said yourself you couldn't understand why they were holding back. They are interested in us, that's all," Leah said almost smugly.

"I know now why they've held back. Your morning prayer service circle," Fargo told her.

"Very good. You are recognizing the power of prayer," Leah said.

"That's not the reason. They've been watching every day, waiting to see what magic comes out of your morning circle," Fargo explained. "The Shoshoni circle is where the medicine man works his magic, and afterward there are war dances and then they go into battle or take the long winter trek or whatever. They've been watching you, wondering, waiting, trying to understand what the hell kind of magic your morning prayer circle had. They've held back out of caution and curiosity, but now they've decided your morning circle hasn't

146

any magic power in it at all. Nothing happens after it. They've decided there's no need to be careful any longer. They're going to attack."

Leah met his answer with an appraising gaze. "What have you found out about the money?" she asked.

"Nothing, yet," he snapped.

It was Shadrach's voice that spoke up. "Maybe Brother Fargo is in such a hurry to see us flee here so he can have the money for himself," the man said.

"Maybe you're a stupid ass," Fargo said.

"Would you do that, Fargo?" Leah asked.

"I do not have your faith in this man, Sister Leah," Mishach put in, and Fargo heard the mutter of agreement from the others as they circled him.

"You're all fools. What I'd do or not do doesn't mean a damn thing. The Shoshoni are going to attack," Fargo threw back. "Forget the girl, and the money, and save your damn skins."

"Give me your gun, Fargo," Leah said, and Fargo stared at her. He half-turned to see Zach Kurtz behind him with a heavy Walker Colt trained on his back. At his right, Mishach had a gun on him, and at his left, Shadrach, Zeb Classoon, and Eb Carlton had guns on him. He slowly lifted the Colt from its holster and dropped it to the ground, his eyes on Leah.

"She doesn't know where the damn money is hidden," he said.

"She has convinced you to help her. The devil has no trouble finding allies," Leah said. "You are a disappointment to me, Fargo."

"You are a failure to me, honey," he returned.

She flicked a glance at Shadrach, and the man came to him at once, using a length of lariat to tie

147

his wrists together in front of him. Fargo's glance went to Rachel, and he saw dismay and helplessness in her hazel eyes. He let his gaze go past her and felt the rueful smile edge his lips. Being right wasn't always a cause for satisfaction. A line of near-naked horsemen had come halfway down the west hill, and he looked east to see another line of Shoshoni warriors. Leah saw the bitterness in his face and followed his gaze.

"Those look like bluebirds to you?" he asked as a third line of braves materialized on the north hill. Slowly, the three lines began to move down closer to the flatland of the hollow until they halted again.

"They have come to observe. We have nothing to fear and we will show no fear. We shall all go about our usual activities," Leah said.

"Untie me, dammit," Fargo roared. "Get your wagons into a circle. Do something to protect yourselves."

"Can't you understand that we have been sent here, and nothing will harm us?" Leah asked him. "The spirit is with us. Salvation shall be ours."

"Maybe another place and another time. Right now you're going to need six-gun salvation, honey," Fargo threw back at her.

"Why are you so certain the Shoshoni will attack, Fargo?" Leah asked almost chidingly.

He eyed her grimly. "When you left Rachel, they thought you'd left her as a gift. When I took her back, it was the kind of insult that has to be avenged," he told her.

Leah's eyes darkened as she stared at him severely. "Then you had no right to take her back," she accused.

"You'd no goddamn right to leave her in the first place," Fargo fired back.

Leah looked away and frowned into space for a moment. When she turned back, her eyes went to Mishach and Shadrach as the two men stood by. Fargo saw the light of righteous triumph come into her face.

"The answer is given us, and it is called Rachel," Leah intoned. "We shall just give the gift back again."

"What?" Fargo barked incredulously.

Leah's glance went to the two men, and Shadrach started for Rachel.

Fargo lifted his bound wrists and rushed at Leah. "You crazy bitch," he shouted. The blow from Mishach caught him across the back of the neck, and he fell forward onto his knees, went down on his side as Mishach's kick slammed into his ribs.

"No," he heard Rachel scream, but Shadrach had her by both arms. Mishach went to his aid as she kicked and tried to bite.

"Bind her. Take a tent stake," Leah ordered, and Fargo pulled himself onto his knees as Zach Kurtz fished a stake from his wagon.

"It won't work now," Fargo yelled at Leah. "They won't take her now. They'll see it as a bribe not a gift, dammit." He struggled to his feet and tried to rush at Leah again, but this time Zeb Classoon seized him and flung him to the ground. Fargo held his tied wrists to one side to avoid a broken arm as he fell. "You can't do this, dammit," he shouted again at Leah. "It won't work. You're just sacrificing her for nothing."

"To offer a sacrifice for a greater good is permitted," Leah answered.

Fargo swore, and Zeb Classoon and Zach Kurtz lifted him to his feet as Shadrach and Mishach dragged Rachel from the campsite. Mishach held the tent stake in one hand, and the two men pulled the girl along between them until they reached a place not far from the end of the hollow along the west hillside. They hammered the stake into the ground and tied Rachel to it hand and foot.

"You bastards," Fargo spit out. "You twisted-up, hypocritical bastards."

Leah turned to glance at him. "Tie him to that wagon wheel," she said, and Fargo was dragged to the rear wheel of one of the Conestogas. With his wrists still bound together, he was strapped against the wheel, where he could clearly see Rachel tied to the stake. He heard her scream as Mishach and Shadrach left her, pleading and protest mingled in her voice. His eyes went to the hillside, where the line of Shoshoni watched.

He saw Leah turn to him. "They understand," she said. "They are content to look on."

"They've no reason to hurry. They can afford to take their time and let you sweat it out," Fargo told her.

"They will come down and claim their gift again," Leah said.

"Shit they will," Fargo muttered, saw Preacher Thomas come to stand nearby, his eyes on the figure of Rachel at the stake. "You stand by and let them do this to your daughter, you weasel," Fargo said.

The man's eyes were saucers of weakness as he stared back at him. His voice was tired, his words delivered with apologetic hesitancy. "I could not stop them. They wouldn't have listened to me," he murmured.

"You didn't even try," Fargo hissed. The man turned away to trudge head-down back to his wagon. Fargo's eyes went to the west hillside nearest the stake, and he scanned the line of Shoshoni. Three had left, their places empty as the others remained motionless. He frowned, uncertain of what it meant but sure it boded no good for Rachel. He turned his eyes to her and saw that she sagged against the stake, her round face drawn in with fear and pain.

Fargo scanned the campsite. Delia Tooner and the Spencer woman were washing clothes in a wooden bucket filled with water. Zach Kurtz sat by his wagon cleaning his rifle. The Tooner and Spencer kids played games, and Ruth Classoon darned socks. Shadrach and Mishach lounged beside one of the Conestogas, and Leah rested outside her wagon and looked righteously confident. They all seemed supremely unconcerned, and Fargo cursed under his breath. Somehow, he had to get free, he realized. Somehow he had to get to Rachel before it was too late.

His fingers opened and closed, curled against his trouser leg. He could reach the double-edged knife in the calf holster if he had the time. But they'd see him. He had to wait for dark. If only the Shoshoni would spare him the time, he muttered. He peered across at the line of red men and cursed. They still waited motionlessly, and his eyes went to the sky. The sun had moved quickly and was more than halfway to the horizon, he saw. He settled back and fought down the terrible desire to try to reach the holster around his calf.

The others were going about their chores, and his gaze bored into Leah with a hate that surprised him. He had underestimated the power of her convictions, twisted or not. Or maybe he had just overestimated the power of the body. He saw her straighten, frown into the distance, and he followed her gaze.

The three Shoshoni had returned, and Fargo watched them move down onto the flatland of the hollow. They slowly advanced toward Rachel, one carrying a goatskin gourd. They dismounted when they reached her, and Fargo caught the panic in Rachel's eyes. Two stepped to her and began to rip her clothes from her until she was naked except for a few shredded strips of cloth. The Indian with the gourd came forward and poured the contents over her, and Fargo heard Rachel's whimpered cry.

Leah half-ran toward the wagon wheel. "What are they doing?" she asked. "What are they pouring over her?"

Fargo peered across the distance, straining his vision as he concentrated on Rachel's round nakedness. The Shoshoni with the gourd had stepped back, and Fargo watched the liquid he had poured over the girl slowly move down her body, slide over her lovely, round high breasts, trickle down across her round little belly. He might have smiled in other circumstances. It always felt good to be right. Only now it made him sick inside. He met Leah's frown. "Honey," he said.

"What?" Leah questioned.

"That's what they poured over her. Honey," Fargo bit out.

"Why? What does it mean?" Leah pressed.

"When it gets dark and grizzlies will be out prowling for food. They'll smell the honey for miles and come after it. When they find it, they'll tear Rachel apart piece by piece for it," he said.

"Why are they doing this?" She frowned.

"They're telling you what they think about your gift. They're giving it to the bears. They're showing you their contempt by that," Fargo told her and the others that had gathered around to listen. "They'll stay there and put an arrow through anybody that tries to save her. And tonight, you can listen to her screams as the grizzlies tear at her. By tomorrow maybe you'll be too unnerved to put up any kind of a fight."

"The savages," Leah said sternly.

"They didn't put her out there," Fargo said, and Leah's eyes blazed at him.

"Are you putting me in the same class as those heathens?" she flung at him.

"No, they're more honest about it," he returned. He managed to turn his head and took Leah's blow along the side of his face.

"The devil sent you, Fargo," she hissed, then she whirled and strode to her wagon.

Fargo lifted his head, peered across the hollow as the dusk began to roll down the hills. Rachel sagged against the stake, and he saw the deerflies already buzzing around her. Beyond, the Shoshoni waited, motionless, and Fargo beckoned the night with silent prayer. He would have but a few hours at best under cover of the darkness. He had to reach Rachel before the grizzlies.

He settled back and watched the women prepare supper as the darkness finally came. The meal was taken in the usual silence, and he saw that they really had no fear. They truly believed they would remain unharmed. His thoughts went to Diane. She should have been able to slip away from the house under the cloak of dusk. Perhaps she'd be the only one to come out of this alive, he reflected.

The disciples faded into their wagons, and the camp grew still. Fargo reached down and pulled his trouser leg up with the fingers of his bound hands. He got a grip on the hilt of the thin knife and drew it from its holster. He turned the hilt carefully until he had the blade pointed upward and his fingers had a frim grip on the knife. Slowly, he began to cut the ropes that bound his wrists. His fingers cramped quickly, and he had to rest often, but he continued to saw at the ropes. It seemed an endless task made of painful slowness, but he knew he had made some progress by the tiny shreds of rope that fell onto his wrists.

He suddeuly heard footsteps and quietly dropped the blade down between his legs. He rested his head back against the wagon wheel as Mishach halted before him. Satisfied the ropes were still in place, the man went back to the other side of the camp.

Fargo swore as he fished down between his legs until he grasped the knife again. Once more he had to work it around in his fingers till he had a firm grip on it, and he felt the line of perspiration coating his brow. Precious time continued to slip away as he began cutting the ropes once more. He fought down the pain of cramped fingers and sawed at the ropes, swore as they refused to give way. When he finally had to halt to relax his fingers, he peered up into the night sky. Clouds allowed only a fitful moon to peek through, and he was grateful for that much. With a silent roar of frustration, he attacked the ropes again. He had just felt the ropes begin to give when his wildcat's hearing picked up the slow, shuffling sound that was unmistakably bear.

He yanked at the ropes, stretching his powerful forearm muscles, and with a soundless snap the ropes gave way. He twisted, enough room now for him to work the knife, and severed the ropes that bound him to the wagon wheel with a half-dozen swift strokes. He pulled himself up to a crouch, flexed his fingers as he scanned the dark. The camp was silent, everyone inside their wagons. But not asleep, he wagered, each waiting for Rachel's screams to pierce the night.

The Shoshoni also waited on the hillside, too far from the stake to see under the fitful moon. But they could hear, and by now they had picked up the sounds of the grizzly drawing near. Fargo paused as he saw the Ovaro tied to the Classoons' seed-bed wagon. The Ovaro would get him to the stake faster, but the sound of hoofprints would bring the Shoshoni charging, and that would only mean another kind of death for Rachel and himself. He had to free her without the Indians knowing, and he started to race across the hollow on foot.

He dug his heels into the ground as he ran with all the speed his powerful long legs could give him. He could smell the grizzly now as his nostrils picked up the powerful, pungent odor. Grizzlies always smelled bad, their strong odor unmistakable. With the wind right, you could smell a bear a hundred yards away. But this one was no hundred yards away, and the smell of him was almost overpowering. Rachel came into sight at the same instant as the huge bulk of the grizzly. Fargo saw the bear lumber toward the stake with the swinging gait that let him sniff the air in all directions as he moved. He was only a few yards from Rachel.

Fargo drove forward, went into a long, loping

crouch. He reached Rachel just as the bear did, and he saw Rachel see him through eyes of pure terror.

"Help me. Oh, God, help me," she murmured in a desperate whisper, and he saw her turn her head away, shrink back against the ropes that held her as she felt the putrid breath of the big bear on her face. "Oh, my God," Rachel gasped.

The bear paused in front of the honey smell, his massive head swinging from side to side. Fargo saw no sign that the huge animal was even aware of his presence as the bear concentrated on the sweet smell that had brought him there. Fargo circled to come up behind Rachel, the thin-bladed knife in his hand. It would be useless to throw the knife, he knew. The blade would hardly penetrate the dense coat, much less the thick skin of the bear, and Fargo heard Rachel's scream as the bear swept his tongue across her breasts and tasted the honey. Fargo cursed as he dropped to one knee and cut the first set of ropes, came up with the knife, and severed the second set.

Only one more to go, and he cast a glance at the huge form of the bear. Rachel's screams had made the bear pause for a moment, but Fargo saw the grizzly slowly raise one huge paw. He cursed as he severed the last set of ropes binding Rachel to the stake. But the grizzly's paw was coming down in a short arc, and Fargo winced himself as he saw the five-inch nails rip through Rachel's shoulder as though it was made of paper.

Rachel's scream of pain split the night as—the ropes that bound her severed—she sank to the ground at the base of the stake. Fargo saw the bear swing the giant paw in another swipe, hit the stake, and knock it to the side as though it had been a hollow reed. Rachel lay on the ground, and

Fargo saw the grizzly bend his head, bring his big snout half under her, and flip her over, much the way he did with a salmon scooped from a stream. Rachel had fainted, Fargo saw, and he knew that her silence probably saved her from the terrible fangs that would have torn into her in reaction to another scream.

Fargo shoved the thin blade into his belt and reached down, picked up the stake as the bear's tongue took another long lick across her honey-smeared body. It would be only another few moments before the grizzly closed his jaws around her body to carry off his prize, and Fargo stepped forward, holding the long thick stake as if it were a club.

He brought it around in a long arc and sent it crashing into the grizzly's rump. With a roar more of surprise than pain, the bear swung his massive bulk around, focusing his little eyes on the intruder. The grizzly started to lumber toward him, and Fargo knew the slowness was dangerously deceptive. He brought the stake around and held it as a lance this time.

The grizzly moved closer and Fargo stepped back, feinted to the left, and saw the bear's eyes follow him. He backed once more, and the giant form came forward faster. The grizzly had fantastic power and strength, the massive bulk supported on legs thick as small trees, shoulders so huge they could withstand anything but a perfect hit with a rifle bullet. There was only one place he could strike, Fargo knew, and he half-circled, feinted again with his stake held in front of him. He wanted the grizzly to charge. He needed a single split second, and he'd only have one chance, he knew. He drove the stake forward, thrust it into the huge chest, and felt himself bounce backward as the grizzly continued to advance.

He ducked down, brought the stake up lance-fashion, and caught the bear alongside the head. The grizzly ignored the blow, but his paw lashed out with that deceptive speed, and Fargo felt the stake fly out of his grasp. He dived sideways as the grizzly lunged forward, swiping a paw at him, but missing. Fargo hit the ground, rolled, and retrieved the stake as the bear swung around to face him again. He heard a low growl rumble from the huge chest. The grizzly was beginning to get angry.

Fargo came at him again, letting his own body follow the swinging head, and he lunged forward with a quick, sudden motion. He hit the bear on the end of the snout with the stake, and the grizzly roared in anger, rearing up on his hind legs to all but blot out the sky. The bear took two steps forward, came down on all fours, and lunged again. Fargo, his powerful muscles knotted in readiness, saw the paw swipe at him, but he was ready for it. He dropped low, and the huge paw swept air over his head. Fargo drove the stake upward with all his might, leaping forward much as a pole-vaulter would. He plunged the end of the stake into the grizzly's left eye, dropped to the ground, and rolled. This time the bear's roar was made of excruciating pain as well as rage, and the grizzly swung his huge form away, lowered his head, and pawed at his injured eye.

Fargo came up on his feet and raced for Rachel's unconscious form. He picked her up, put her over his shoulder, and cursed at the deep slashes that poured blood down her body. He began to run with her, using a long, loping stride that kept her across his shoulder with the least amount of jouncing. He glanced back to see the grizzly still pawing at his eye, and Fargo ran toward the little hill at the other end of the hollow.

Rachel's screams and the bear's bellowing were more than enough to satisfy the Shoshoni that their savage gesture had gone off as expected. Leah was undoubtedly holding a prayer session that invoked mercy as it deplored the price of sin. Fargo spat in disgust as he ran. They'd all be learning about the price of sin and stupidity come morning.

He slowed as he started up the hill, his calf muscles protesting. Rachel was still unconscious on his shoulder. He reached the top and headed for the open doorway of the darkened house. He had just reached it when a figure came into view in the doorway. "In here, on the mattress," Diane said.

"What the hell are you doing here? I told you to go to the caves," Fargo barked as he carried Rachel inside, laying her gently down on the mattress.

"I couldn't make it. Too many Shoshoni crossing the hills behind me," she told him. "I decided to wait here until morning. I could see what was happening below until it got dark. God, I never felt so helpless in my life." Diane lit a little candle that gave enough light to send a soft glow through the room.

Fargo leaned over Rachel, whose breathing was becoming steady. Her torn shoulder was bloody and raw in the candlelight. "Water," he muttered. "We've got to clean this wound."

Diane fetched a big basin of water and cloths

and helped wash the sticky honey from Rachel as Fargo cleansed the deep wounds as best he could.

"I've some yarrow poultices," Diane said as he tore a sheet into bandage strips.

"Get them," Fargo said. There was nothing better for cuts than the yarrow, and he applied the poultices carefully over each long gash.

Diane helped him bandage them in place, then brought a blouse and skirt, and dressed the still-unconscious girl.

Suddenly Fargo called out. "She's waking," he said as Rachel's eyes fluttered. She stirred and her eyes opened, and he saw terror in their hazel depths. She tried to sit up but fell back in pain. "It's all right, honey," Fargo said, and the terror slowly faded from her eyes. Diane fetched a jigger of bourbon, and he held Rachel up as she sipped it.

"My shoulder, it's on fire," she gasped.

"It'll stay that way a good while. You've some nasty tears," Fargo told her, and Rachel finished the bourbon and closed her eyes. She fell back on the mattress, asleep almost instantly.

"I heard it. I could only imagine her being torn apart. I threw up," Diane said as she sank down beside him and blew out the candle. "What kind of people would leave her to the Shoshoni? They must be monsters, not missionaries." Diane shuddered.

Fargo saw the pink-gray light of dawn seeping in through the open doorway and stood up. "We'll talk about it later," he said.

Diane walked to the door with him. He could see the wagons in the hollow, and his eyes swept the hillsides. The Shoshoni had moved down from the hills and were at the edge of the flatland. As he watched, they slowly began to converge on the wagons. Fargo saw the figures emerge from the wagons, Leah striding to the center of the campsite. The others gathered around her and dropped to their knees for the morning prayer service.

Fargo lay down on the ground and drew Diane down beside him.

"What's the matter with them? They're not even trying to defend themselves." She frowned.

"Shades of Reverend Johnston," Fargo murmured, and Diane frowned again. "I told him God doesn't reward stupidity," Fargo bit out. Suddenly, he heard a sound behind him. He whirled and saw Rachel moving out of the doorway on unsteady legs. He reached up and pulled her down beside Diane and saw her stare down at the hollow, her lips parted, her eyes haunted. "I think you'd best go inside," he said gently.

"No," Rachel murmured. "No."

Fargo half-shrugged. Maybe she deserved that much, he grunted. His eyes swept the Shoshoni as they sent their ponies into a slow trot, each rider pulling back on his bow, arrows all in place. He didn't see the signal, but the hail of arrows filled the air from all sides. His eyes were on the prayer circle.

Four arrows hurtled into Leah, one pinning her folded hands against her breasts. Other figures in the circle toppled forward, and he saw still others leap up and start to race for their wagons. But the Shoshoni were in full attack from all sides, and though he'd neither the time nor the desire to count, he didn't think any of the racing figures reached the wagons.

The Shoshoni had swept into the campsite from every side, leaping from their ponies to plunder bodies and wagons. It had taken only moments, hardly enough time to say amen, Fargo thought ironically. The Trailsman rose, bitterness all over his face, and pulled Diane and Rachel to their feet. The Shoshoni would be busy for a while now, plundering first, then burning the wagons.

"Now's our chance. Let's move," he muttered.

Diane had described the two caves accurately. They were tall, narrow, clean, and well-hidden. He had carried Rachel most of the way, and now he sat beside her. Diane sat across from him in the narrow, dark hiding place. Rachel's round face was full of pain, and her eyes sought his, a terrible lostness in them.

"Is it all nothing, Fargo?" Rachel asked. "Believing, faith, the power of the Word—is it all meaningless?"

"No, can't say that," Fargo answered.

"None of it worked for them," Rachel said.

"Faith's one thing. Stupidity's another," he answered. "But mostly they were twisted and misguided, believers who turned believing into something it was never meant to be. They were idiots with an ideal. All they had was the faith of fools. They lost sight of what it's all supposed to mean. Or maybe they never had hold of it."

Rachel nodded, then closed her eyes. She fell quickly into a deep sleep, and Fargo felt Diane's eyes on him.

"That was nice," she commented, and he frowned back. "The answer you gave her," she explained.

"It was rough for her. She needs something left to hang on to," he said.

"You sounded as though you meant it," Diane said.

"I did," he answered as he rose and walked to the cave entrance. He edged his way out, scanned the nearby terrain, listened, stepped farther out, and sniffed the air. When he reentered the cave, he fastened his eyes on Diane.

"They burned the house. The smell of it's still in the air," he said, and she shrugged ruefully. "What did you bring with you?" he asked.

"Some extra clothes, my ointment, and all my work with my sketch pad," she said, and gestured to the soft cloth bag on the floor of the cave.

"I figure the Shoshoni will race around for a few hours more, then simmer down and go back to their camp," Fargo said.

"That's when we try to get away," Diane said, and he saw surprise in her eyes as he shook his head.

"My Ovaro's out there someplace. So's my Colt and my Sharps. They're all part of me. I'm not going without them," he told her. "You need a mount, too."

"I'd rather walk alive than ride dead," Diane said. "Seems to me you're pushing your luck."

"Luck's mostly what you make it," he said as he sank down on the floor of the cave beside her.

Diane drew his head across her lap, and her hand stroked his forehead. "Sleep some. I know you need it," she said, and he nodded agreement. He closed his eyes and enjoyed the softness of her lap as he let sleep sweep over him.

He slept heavily, and when he woke, the tall

cave had grown warm from the midday sun. He rose, looked across at Rachel's sleeping form.

"She's been tossing and turning restlessly, and she cries out in pain every time," Diane said.

"I'll be back as fast as I can," Fargo said.

Diane got to her feet and pressed her lips against his. "To make sure you'll be careful," she said.

He tossed her a tired smile and edged from the cave. Once again, his eyes swept the terrain as he moved out to the base of the little hill in the hollow. The charred odor still hung in the air. He moved forward in a crouch. He could see the burned wagons when he reached the front of the hill, and spotted the Ovaro in the background, the horse grazing at the edge of the trees. Two other horses moved aimlessly at the edges of the campsite,

Fargo moved forward in his long, loping gait and slowed as he reached the edge of the campsite. He walked determinedly into the space at the center of the charred wagons and began to pick his way among the arrow-riddled bodies that lay grotesquely throughout the campsite like so many broken doll figures.

He forced himself to search for the things he wanted, refusing to see the bodies as names, individuals, entities. He found his Colt on the ground beside an outstretched hand, searched further, and spotted his rifle half under one of the blackened wagons. He retrieved both weapons, turned quickly, and almost stumbled over a figure at his feet. He glimpsed the deep-blond hair and turned away immediately toward where the Ovaro grazed. The horse trotted to him when he called it, and he gathered the reins of a brown mare nearby and led both horses away, skirting the edge of the low hill once more. He halted halfway to the cave and let his eyes carefully scan the surrounding hills. Satisfied the Shoshoni were not watching, he continued on.

He reached the cave and led both horses inside.

Diane hugged him to her. "I was so afraid. I kept pacing back and forth," she murmured. "I kept thinking of your luck running out."

"I told you, luck's mostly what you make it," he said. "It'll be dark in a few hours. We'll travel by night, sleep by day, at least till we're out of the Painted Hills." He glanced over at Rachel as she turned in her sleep and cried out in pain. He kept the stab of apprehension to himself, but he knew that his cleansing of her terrible gashes had been makeshift, at best, and that bear claws carried all manner of infectious things. He sat down against one wall of the cave, and Diane folded herself in front of him.

"You think any about the money?" he asked her.

"No," she said.

"Going to forget about it?" he queried.

"There's nothing else to do. I haven't been able to think of anything that'd tell us where it is. I don't really want it. It's brought only grief," Diane said soberly.

"Maybe you're right," Fargo agreed. "But it's a hell of a lot of money to walk away from."

"My plate's already full." Diane half-smiled. "My pa liked to say that to me."

"What'd he mean?" Fargo asked.

She shrugged. "I never knew exactly. It just seemed a favorite expression of his. 'Your plate's already full, take it from Charley Keller,' he used to say to me. I took it to mean that he felt I already had plenty of good things in life."

Fargo frowned as he turned the phrase over in his mind with prodding insistence. "What if it was more than just an expression?" he mused aloud as he felt a stab of excitement dig at him. "What if it meant something more?" he continued.

"Such as?" Diane said.

"What kind of a plate do you think of as being full or empty?" Fargo returned, and the excitement spiraled inside him now. "You don't think of a soup plate or a dinner plate in that way," he said. "You think of a collection plate. A collection plate is either full or empty." He paused and watched realization slowly flood Diane's face.

"The stone altar," she said breathlessly. "At the side, that stone shaped just like a collection plate."

"Bull's-eye," Fargo said. "That's where he hid the money."

Fargo watched Diane stare thoughtfully at him. "Let it stay there," she finally said. "You got away going back once. Don't try it again. Don't tempt fate."

"Hell, I've made a career of that." He grinned. "Besides, somebody ought to get something good out of all that's happened. Why not you?"

"And you and Rachel. We can share it," Diane said, her face brightening for an instant before becoming grave again. "But I'm still afraid, Fargo."

"I'll be back," he said as he rose.

Diane jumped to her feet with him. "No, you're not going alone. I can't stay here waiting. I almost went mad the last time. I don't care how dangerous it is. It'll be better than staying here." He cast a glance at Rachel. "She'll stay asleep till we get back," Diane said.

"Get on the horse. We've a couple of hours of

daylight left," he said, and swung onto the Ovaro. "We'll exchange speed for caution."

He sent the pinto out of the cave in a fast canter, Diane close behind him. They went into a full gallop when they reached the flatland of the hollow and slowed only when they reached the big stone altar. Fargo leapt from the saddle and ran to the concave-shaped stone at the end of the flat stone. Diane beside him, he peered at all sides of the piece of stone, saw nothing to break the smooth surface. He tried to shake the entire piece and found it impossible.

"Maybe we guessed wrong," Diane muttered, but Fargo crouched down and began to run his fingers along the underside of the plate-shaped piece. He was halfway around when he halted.

"I feel something," he said, and bent down to see a thin crack running along the underside of the stone. He pressed hard against the stone at the other side of the crack. "It's moving," he called out. "Hot damn, it's moving."

He pressed harder and the piece loosened further until suddenly it swung in at one side to give him enough room to grasp hold of it. He pulled and a section of the underside of the platelike formation of stone came out in his hands. He stared into the hollowed-out section of stone. Little shreds of what had been a burlap sack littered the surface along with a small mound of dry, crumbly bits of paper. He cast a glance at Diane, saw her frowning down at the stone.

"What is it?" she murmured.

He almost laughed. But all he could muster was a wry, bitter sound. "Twenty thousand dollars," he said. "All that's left of it." Diane frowned at him. "Your pa picked a great hiding place, but he didn't think of one thing. Fifteen years of sun baking down. It made this little section of hollowed-out stone into an oven. Little by little, over the years, it just dried out the money, dried it into dust and these little scraps of paper."

"All for nothing," she said. "All of them chasing after nothing."

Fargo pushed the piece of stone back in place in the underside of the rock formation, secured it into place, and turned. He took Diane by the hand as he walked back to the horses. "Disappointed?" he asked.

"No, strangely enough," she said thoughtfully. "It just wasn't meant to be. It's a kind of a lesson, too. You should be sure of what you go chasing after."

"Damn hard lesson for some," Fargo said, and swung onto the Ovaro. Diane rode back to the cave with him in silence, and when they reached the tall hiding place, they found Rachel sitting up.

"Think we left you?" He laughed.

"I knew better than that," she said, and winced. "My shoulder hurts something fierce."

"We'll change the bandages later. Right now we're going to get out of here," he said. "It's not dark yet, but we might as well get started."

"There's a little stream just behind here. I'm going to fill the canteens," Diane said. He nodded and handed her his canteen, and she hurried from the cave. He turned as she ran back in, her eyes wide with fear.

"Outside." She swallowed hard.

He brushed past her as he headed for the mouth of the cave and peered out. The line of Shoshoni stretched across the face of both caves.

"Shit," he muttered, and turned back into the

cave to see Rachel clinging to Diane, both watching him with eyes wide. "They saw us at the rock and watched us come back here," he said. "Goddamn."

"Is there anything we can do?" Diane asked.

"Fight," Fargo snapped bitterly. "Maybe we can bring down enough of them to make them decide we're not worth bothering with."

"You really think that'll work?" Diane asked.

"No, but I can't see anything else to do," he said.

"I'll go to them," Rachel said. "Maybe they'll take me now and let you two go on."

"No way," Fargo snapped.

"You saved me twice. Maybe it's meant to be this way," Rachel said, pain, weariness, and resignation showing in her round face.

He stared at her, turned her words in his mind. "Maybe it is," he said slowly.

"*Fargo!*" Diane gasped, disbelief in the single word.

"Can you sit a horse alone?" Fargo asked Rachel.

"Maybe, for a few minutes," she answered.

"What are you saying? You can't let her give herself to them for us," Diane protested.

"I haven't time to explain now," he flung at her, and stepped to Rachel. "Get on the Ovaro," he said, half-lifting her into the saddle as she gasped in pain. "Sit tall," he told her. "Fight away the pain. Just sit tall and ride slowly out of here, very slowly." Rachel nodded, and he swung onto the brown mare, motioning to Diane. "Take your things and get on behind me," he said.

Diane whirled, gathered her sketch pad and the soft cloth bag and canteens, and climbed onto the mare behind him. She held on with one arm around his waist.

"Let's go," he said, and Rachel moved the Ovaro forward.

Fargo swung the brown mare in close behind the Ovaro and followed Rachel out of the cave. She rode tall, he saw, and sent silent encouragement to her. She emerged from the cave and Fargo's eyes went to the Shoshoni. He saw them stare at Rachel, their black eyes wide. They exchanged glances of surprise first, then nervousness, then awe. He watched as they moved their ponies back and opened a path for Rachel. The Shoshoni moved back farther on both sides, and Fargo heard their murmured voices behind as he followed Rachel on through the trees. They heard the sound of the ponies galloping away, but he let Rachel go on until the very last sound faded away.

He spurred the mare alongside Rachel, reached out, and caught her as she toppled sideways from the horse. Diane slid from the mare and helped him lower Rachel to the ground.

"You did it, honey," he said to the girl. And Rachel's eyes flickered in answer.

"Now would you mind telling me what that was all about?" Diane demanded.

"Signs," Fargo said.

"Signs?"

"I knew they'd recognize Rachel at once. They'd left her to be killed by the grizzly. They heard her screams, heard the bear kill her. But here she was alive. It was a sign she was a spirit person, a being not to be touched," Fargo said. "Everybody has their signs. Leah had hers. The Shoshoni have theirs."

Diane heard the tinge of bitterness that crept into his voice, and came to him, holding her arms around his neck. "You're a sign, a great big, wonderful sign," she said.

"Let's ride," he told her. "I'll take Rachel."

Diane stepped back and helped him as he put Rachel into the saddle and swung up behind her. Rachel's head fell back against his chest, and she seemed half asleep. Diane pressed her hand to the girl's forehead.

"Fever," she said. "It'll get worse. We've nothing to treat it. We've got to get her to a doctor."

"That means finding a town," Fargo said. "Mount up. We'll be riding day and night." He set off, holding Rachel's limp form against him with the sides of his arms as he sent the Ovaro out of the hollow and onto the narrow trails beyond.

They rested twice during the night, and Diane had been right. Rachel's fever had spiraled, and he let Diane ride with her when morning came. He climbed into the hills and swept the distant land. They halted at a clear, spring pool and bathed Rachel in the cold water as the day wore on. It helped keep the fever from rising further, but he could smell the infection in the deep gashes of her shoulder. He left her with Diane to race up the next high place. It was nearly dark when he caught the distant flicker of light, and he raced back to where Dinae rode slowly along a narrow trail.

"Some kind of town to the east," he said as he led the way, hoping it held a doctor. It was dark when he rode onto a wagon trail. He felt the surge of hope: a wagon trail usually meant a town large enough to have a doctor. The town came into sight, a weathered sign at the outskirts proclaiming the name OWENS CORNERS. He rode ahead again and reined up at a public stable.

"Need a doctor," he called to the stableman who appeared from inside.

"Doc Sawyer, last house at the other end of town," the man said as Fargo saw Diane coming up. He motioned to her as he raced on through the town. He had the doctor awakened and ready as Diane rode up with Rachel. Fargo explained her wounds as the doctor poured disinfectant powder on the deep gashes after cleaning the surface infection away.

"Fever's bad, but not so bad we can't save her," the doctor said when he finished, and put Rachel into a side room in a wide bed. "I'd say you got her here just in time. Another twenty-four hours and that infection would be out of hand."

"We'll stop by tomorrow," Fargo said. "There a boardinghouse around here?"

"Murphy's, middle of town," the doctor said.

Fargo walked the short distance to the boardinghouse and found the place a neat, proper rooming house run by a proper woman named Bridgit Murphy, who automatically gave them separate rooms.

"I'm going to sleep for days." Diane laughed as she went to her room, and he trudged to the second floor. He fell onto the bed, lay there for a spell before he rose, pulled off his clothes, and fell back to plunge into the sleep of the exhausted.

The sun was bright when he woke and dressed, and Mrs. Murphy told him Diane had already gone to visit the doctor. He hurried to the physician's house to find Diane sitting on the edge of the bed, Rachel awake, and Doc Sawyer standing by.

"Amazing recovery so far," the doctor said. "The resilience of the young."

"Rachel's going to stay on here when she's

recovered," Diane told him, and Fargo lifted his eyebrows.

"I've been looking for an assistant, someone to help me with my patients and my bookkeeping," Doc Sawyer filled in. "We had a little talk, Rachel and I, and she'd do just fine."

Fargo looked at Rachel and saw happiness in her eyes as she nodded at him. He leaned down, kissed her on the forehead.

"Thank you for everything, Fargo," Rachel whispered in his ear. "I'll never forget you."

He straightened, patted her round cheek, and Diane followed him out into the sunlight. "You have any special plans?" she asked him with a sidelong glance.

"No."

"Good," she said. "Because I intend to do a lot more of something that starts with an S."

"Sketching?" he said.

"That, too," she answered.

LOOKING FORWARD!
The following is the opening section
from the next novel in the exciting
Trailsman series from Signet:

The Trailsman #48
THE WHITE HELL TRAIL

*1861—Taos Pueblo
northern New Mexico Territory*

The Trailsman stiffened when the ratty-looking blond man entered the cantina. Fargo had been relaxed—as relaxed as he ever permitted himself to be, anyway, which was still more vigilant and attentive than most men when they were trying to remain alert—with a drink in one hand and the warm, slim waist of a *mestizo* girl under the other. Now he drew himself erect, his whipcord frame taut under a rush of sudden tension. He set the glass aside, and his other hand fell unconsciously away from the now forgotten girl. His lake-blue eyes went suddenly cold. There was ice in the look he gave the newcomer.

The girl, affronted, tried to snuggle back against him. Then she saw the look that had come into those coldly flashing eyes. Her hand went to her throat in a gasp of quick fear, and she scuttled away—away from the sense of raw danger that now surrounded this tall, darkly handsome gringo with the lank, black hair and the ready laughter.

Fargo was not even aware of her as she left him. His concentration was total. It was focused solely on the man with the scraggly whiskers and too long uncut and unwashed blond hair.

"Howdy, Adam," someone said, making room for the newcomer at the bar.

The name was a confirmation. But Fargo needed no confirmation.

This was the man he had been seeking. For all the tortured years.

This man was one of them. He had to be.

One of those who had come by stealth to kill and maim and destroy. One of those who had wiped out a family—Skye Fargo's family—and lived to become the object of a vow Fargo raged to the heavens when he discovered the bodies of the only people in the world he truly loved.

And now here the man was. His death would be the culmination of that vow.

Adam Brighton. It was not the name he had been born with. It was not the name he had used that horror-ridden day. But it was one he had used before and now made the mistake of adopting again.

Fargo's jaw muscles clenched so tightly he couldn't swallow. His arms and shoulders ached from strain. Yet to anyone standing more than a pace distant he would have seemed calm, even outwardly casual, as he took a slow step forward and then another.

The Colt's Patent revolver rode at his waist. His hand slid closer to the use-worn butt.

Fargo moved up behind the man who called himself Brighton. He stopped five paces away. Brighton was laughing at something one of his friends had said. He was picking up a mug of foaming native beer.

"Adam Brighton." Fargo's voice rang cold and crisp through the din of many conversations. The cantina fell silent for less than a second, then there was the clatter of falling chairs as men scrambled out of the way. The icy timbre of Fargo's voice was all too easily recognized as a challenge.

The man who called himself Brighton turned. His face, burned by sun and wind, went suddenly pale.

"I heard you were here," Fargo said. "You talked too much in Mora, Brighton. You let them know where you were heading. Not it's time to pay the piper, Brighton."

Brighton began to tremble. A tic fluttered in the corner of his right eye, and his hands were shaky. "I don't know you," he wailed.

"No, you don't," Fargo said agreeably. "But I know you. I've been following you a long time. Now I've found you."

"My . . . you're lookin' for a man named Brighton, mister. That ain't really my name. I swear it ain't."

Fargo's lips parted in a firghtening caricature of a smile. "I know," he whispered. His eyes were cruel now.

"I made a mistake," the man who called himself Brighton quavered. "I know that now, mister. I learnt my lesson. I swear that to you. I wouldn't do it again. Not never."

Fargo barked sharply, a sound that might have been intended as laughter although there was no hint of humor in the bitterness of it. "I know you won't, Brighton," he said.

"Look here, mister," a man standing near Brighton protested. "You cain't do this. The fella made himself a mistake. Hell, man, we all of us make mistakes."

Fargo turned to the stranger. "What I hear is that you're backing him. Is that what you want?"

The friend looked from Fargo to Brighton and back again. For a moment his courage held. But only for a moment. He looked into the tall man's icy-blue eyes. "No," he mumbled. He turned and slipped away into the crowd that had gathered along the side walls of the cantina.

"Well?" Fargo asked.

"I'm beggin' you, mister. Let me go back and serve my time. I'll confess. I swear I will. I won't give you no trouble. You can have the reward."

Reward. As if any amount of money could ever repay Fargo for the losses he had suffered.

How much money would compensate a young man for the loss of the father who had taught him? For the mother who had birthed and suckled him? For the younger brother whose admiration had been embarrassingly, and so often annoyingly, close to worship?

What kind of reward money could wipe out those losses, Fargo wondered bitterly.

Hell, Fargo didn't even know what else this son-of-a-bitch might be wanted for. He didn't care.

What he cared about was that this man paid for the loss of Fargo's family.

The man who called himself Brighton must have seen Fargo's answer in his eyes. Brighton shook all the harder. His mouth worked, but no sounds passed through his lips. He was facing the specter of implacable death. And he knew it.

Fargo stared at him. All the years, all the countless trails, behind him now. Forgotten.

All he could think of was the gunpowder stink in the place that had once been a happy home. His nostrils were filled with the remembered odors of gunsmoke and fresh blood.

He stared at the man and remembered all of it.

So many times, beside so many campfires, he had looked forward to this moment. It was almost as if Skye Fargo had already lived through this moment ten thousand times before.

Brighton was standing there with a revolver at his belt. Fargo studied him intently. There was a bald spot on the back of the man's head Fargo could not see because of his hat. But he knew it was there.

There would be a scar under that filthy shirt. Fargo had been told about that scar. The dimpled pucker of a long-ago bullet. Someone had shot the man once, nearly killed him. Fargo did not know but had always secretly hoped that it was his father who had holed the son-of-a-bitch.

Fargo sensed the movement before he saw it, and he turned in time to see Brighton's friend, in a surge of courage, swinging a chair at him.

The Trailsman ducked, the chair glancing the top of his head. The blow was not serious, but it caused him to lose his balance, and he went sprawling across the floor. He lay on his back looking into the barrel of Brighton's revolver.

Brighton was peering down at him nervously, his thumb fumbling at the spur of the hammer. "You ain't takin' me back now, mister."

Fargo took a chance. He kicked the chair he'd been hit with and that now lay at his feet. The momentary distraction was all he needed as he pulled the Colt from his holster and aimed it at the blond man standing over him.

The big Colt bellowed, the force of the exploding gunpowder rocking the use-polished walnut grips into the web of Fargo's fist.

Flame and smoke and superheated lead spat from the muzzle. The heavy pellet of hot lead smashed into Adam Brighton's belly.

Brighton staggered. His mouth gaped open in shock and pain, and he doubled over, the Remington in his hand forgotten.

The revolver fell from suddenly nerveless fingers. It hit the floor muzzle down, the impact tripping the hammer and causing the gun to discharge. The force of the unintended explosion sent the revolver dancing crazily into the air.

Brighton went down. He lay on the floor, hunched into himself with both hands clasped to his shattered gut.

"Jesus," someone murmured. "So fast . . ."

Brighton moaned. The Remington lay beside him. Fargo stepped forward and used the side of his boot to sweep the Remington out of reach.

The man who called himself Adam Brighton was dying. He lay on the floor and looked up at his killer with pain-wracked eyes. His lips moved. He had to try three times to get the single word out, and when it did come there was a trickle of blood that accompanied it.

"Why?"

"You ask me that? You know why." Fargo knelt beside Brighton, his expression as hard as a face carved in stone.

For the first time in years he softly spoke the name that once had been his, the name he had carried from his birth until the time of his rebirth, until he took the name Fargo as a reminder of the father who had died because of his employment by Wells, Fargo.

Brighton looked at Fargo blankly. "Never . . . never kilt them, mister. Never even heard of them." He gasped out then shuddered, as his eyes began to glaze.

"Shit." Fargo felt a numbness spreading inside him now, replacing the fury that had been driving him.

He reached forward and swept Brighton's hat off his head.

Brighton's hair was full and thick. *There was no bald patch.*

Fargo rolled Brighton onto his back and ripped his shirt open. Looking for the scar that *had* to be there. *There was no scar.*

"No!" Fargo cried out.

He rose to his feet, turned, and stumbled blindly away.

The alias. The description. The hatred. They had all been accurate. They had been right.

He had come to Taos in search of the man who

called himself Adam Brighton. He had been forced to kill him but he would've killed him anyway, Fargo knew. And he had been the wrong man. The man who had helped to slaughter Fargo's family still walked free and cocky in the world.

There was the bitter taste of bile in Fargo's throat. He felt suddenly worn and sluggish.

He stumbled to the bar and groped on its surface for a glass someone had left there. He raised the glass to his lips and tossed it down without tasting the fiery burn of it.

The girl who had been with him before saw the pain in his eyes and she reached for him. Taking him by the arm, she led him outside. He followed blindly from the cantina into the cold of the winter's night.

She took him around behind the cantina to a line of daub and wattle jacales that had been built within sight of the tall, walled pueblo that once had been the focus of Taos's existence.

She took him inside and wrapped her arms around this handsome trembling *yanqui*. Instinct replaced reason, and her instinct was to give comfort to the big, black-haired, suddenly unsure American.

She pressed him down onto her cot and left him for a moment to drape the low doorway with a blanket, keeping out the cold and the curious.

When she returned to him she lay beside him, pressing the warmth of her body against him, trying to give him comfort in the only way she knew how.

They shared no common language, this dark man and she, but none was needed.

Deft fingers stripped his clothing away and then her own.

Naked, she covered him with blankets and crawled under the coverings at his side, pressing herself against him.

His body was hard. He bore old scars on his flesh. He bore new ones, she knew, in his heart.

She gave him her warmth and the comfort of her arms. For reasons she did not try to understand her heart ached for him. Tears came to her eyes.

She could not speak to him of the wisdom she had learned from both her peoples, so she gave him the only comfort she knew.

She took him in her hands, her touch bringing forth the arousal of his animal maleness.

He grew hard under her touch, and she smiled to herself at the size and strength of him there.

She spoke to him softly in her own tongue. She knew he would not comprehend. It did not matter. The softness of the words and the heat of her touch were enough.

She draped a full thigh over his legs, pressing against him, and raised herself to cover and straddle him.

The man lay quiet and still beneath her, as if uncaring, but his responses told her that he was aware now of her presence. She smiled and reached down between his belly and hers to guide him into position. Then she lowered herself onto him, impaling herself on the spear of his manhood.

Her eyes, a soft and liquid brown, widened with pleasure as she filled herself with him.

Skye Fargo's eyes slowly regained their focus,

and he seemed to be aware of where and what he
was.

His hands fumbled for her, uncertainly at first,
then with purpose as he felt the slim planes of her
back, the warmth and texture of her dusky skin.
His hands slid around to the front to cup one soft
breast and then the other.

He found her nipples, large and very dark, and
rolled them between thumb and forefinger.

The girl moaned and began to move her hips,
providing the impetus that he still lacked.

Fargo sighed and pulled her down closer so he
could take one nipple and then the other between
his lips. He nipped lightly at them, and they
became harder, elongating slightly in response to
him. She moaned again and began to move faster
and more insistantly.

"Yes," Fargo whispered. It was the first he had
spoken since the shock of the discovery, and she
was glad for it. Without understanding the reasons
for his behavior, she knew that he was wounded
somewhere deep inside his soul.

Fargo pulled her down against his chest and
wrapped his arms around her, holding her very
tight for long minutes, not allowing her to move.

Then, he took command of her.

He held her to him and rolled over so that he
was on top of her, still socketed deep within the
heat of her body. He nuzzled the sensitive hollow
at the side of her neck and began to pump slowly
and gently in and out.

She opened herself to him, welcoming the
growing intensity of his thrusts, knowing without
words that this was necessary and good.

Fargo raised himself from her far enough that he could see her eyes. She looked into them deeply, blue eyes—warm and alive once again—probing into her own brown ones, and she smiled.

Fargo smiled back at her and bent to kiss her. The soft mounds of her breasts were warm against him. The grip of her thighs was tight around him. And the pull of her sex surrounding his shaft was hot and welcoming.

"Thank you," he said, knowing that she would understand the sound if not the words.

She said something to him in a language that was not Spanish, then began to move, raising her body to him and falling away again.

Fargo began to respond to her stroking, assuming control now and thrusting with deep, powerful, demanding plunges.

He watched and felt with pleasure as her breath quickened and her gaze became remote, turning inward and concentrating on the sensations that were building inside her loins.

There was a matching rise of pleasurable pressure in him, and he mated his pace and his responses to hers, waiting for her to build with him.

The speed of their coupling quickened. His breathing came faster and faster, and the sweat from his chest gathered warm and slick between her breasts.

He pumped furiously into her now. She clutched frantically with her arms, and her quivering thighs bucked beneath him, seeking to draw ever more of him into herself.

Her eyes closed, and she bit at her underlip with

white, small teeth as her head arched backward until the sinews at her throat stood out sharply under the brown skin.

"Aieee!"

She shuddered and stiffened beneath him, and Fargo let go of his control, allowing the hot, joyous fluids to gush and spew from his body deep into hers.

Fargo trembled slightly from the intensity of it. Then he collapsed onto her, exhausted, drained more from spent emotions than from the joining of man with woman.

He lay there, panting, feeling the sweat trickle from his armpits to drop onto her body.

Eventually he rolled off of her, but held her close, drawing comfort from the nearness of her and the feel of her flesh against his.

And eventually his hand crept out to tangle his fingers in the dark, curling bush of her pubic hair.

This time the impetus and the desire were his, and the girl smiled as she opened herself to receive him again.

Ⓢ

Exciting Westerns by Jon Sharpe

Prices higher in Canada

Buy them at your local
bookstore or use coupon
on last page for ordering.

Ⓢ

SIGNET Brand Westerns You'll Enjoy

**Buy them at your local
bookstore or use coupon
on next page for ordering.**

Ⓢ

SIGNET Double Westerns You'll Enjoy

Other Signet Westerns for you to enjoy